# AFRIKA

## COLLEEN CRAIG

TUNDRA BOOKS

Published in Canada by Tundra Books,
75 Sherbourne Street, Toronto, Ontario M5A 2P9

Published in the United States by Tundra Books of Northern New
York, P.O. Box 1030, Plattsburgh, New York 12901

Library of Congress Control Number: 2007927389

**Library and Archives Canada Cataloguing in Publication**

Craig, Colleen, 1956–
Afrika / Colleen Craig.

ISBN 978-0-88776-807-1

1. South Africa – History – Juvenile fiction. 2. South Africa.
Truth and Reconciliation Commission – Juvenile fiction. I. Title.

PS8555.R264A64 2008 jC813.'54 C2007-902717-2

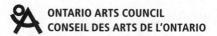

**ONTARIO ARTS COUNCIL
CONSEIL DES ARTS DE L'ONTARIO**

We acknowledge the financial support of the Government of Canada
through the Book Publishing Industry Development Program (BPIDP)
and that of the Government of Ontario through the Ontario Media
Development Corporation's Ontario Book Initiative. We further
acknowledge the support of the Canada Council for the Arts and the
Ontario Arts Council for our publishing program.

Printed and bound in Canada

This book is printed on acid-free paper that is 100% recycled,
ancient-forest friendly (100% post-consumer recycled).

1 2 3 4 5 6     13 12 11 10 09 08

*For Lyndsey and Lauren*

# CONTENTS

# ONE

# HELLO AFRIKA

"Let's go," said Kim as the plane came to a complete stop on the runway.

Her mom, the sort who could not stay still for a moment, sat like a statue beside her. "I can't," she said.

*Oh great*, thought Kim. Passengers jumped to their feet and retrieved their belongings from the overhead bins. Out the airplane's cubbyhole window, Kim watched a staircase being pushed up against the plane. Sooner or later Kim and her mother would have to exit.

"*Riana*," Kim pleaded. She often called her mom by her first name, especially when she was trying to get her attention. "We have to go now." From the pocket of her jean jacket Kim produced a chocolate bar and split it in two. She packed one half into her mouth and waved the other under her mother's nose.

"I swore," Riana said, ignoring the chocolate, "I would never set foot back here again."

Kim was itching to get off the plane. "Do we pack you off to the mental home or what?" Kim was trying to lighten up her mom's mood, but with the thick chocolate in her mouth, her words sounded more sarcastic than usual.

She could not move until her mother got up from the aisle seat. Impatiently Kim folded away the dog-eared map that she had drawn of the plane's tedious nine-hour flight from western Canada to Britain. Tedious with a capital *T*. In London they had changed planes and a thick orange marker highlighted the final grueling twelve-hour stretch across Africa to Cape Town.

Kim had scrawled *Afrika* across the bottom of the page. She had never set foot on this continent; she knew nothing of it except rare snippets from her mother and pictures from *National Geographic*, but she knew Africa was not spelled with a *K*. Still, for some reason the unfamiliar spelling looked right. At least to her blood-shot, jet-lagged eyes. She almost mentioned it to her mother, but Riana was beyond caring at this moment.

Kim checked the deep pocket on the chair in front of her mom to make sure she had everything. "Mom, come on. We have to go."

Kim's mother was a journalist who had investigated many difficult events. She had gone to the Caribbean to cover the stories of people who had lost everything to hurricanes. She had written about survivors of shipwrecks and plane crashes. And she was good at her job. This was why her radio station had sent her to Africa to cover the Truth Commission. Riana could talk to anyone about anything. But whenever Kim questioned her about South Africa, her mother's country of birth, she clammed up as if she had seen a ghost. End of conversation.

Kim tidied up her mom's stuff. Riana liked to wear cool, larger-than-life glasses and, even though she owned three pairs, she misplaced them often. "Remember, I didn't jump for joy about coming here either," said Kim putting her mom's gaudy glasses back in their case.

Even as she spoke these words Kim knew they weren't entirely true. At times she had been so excited about the trip to South Africa that she couldn't sleep. Travel meant adventure – and she loved adventure. Yet, in the three months they would be away from Canada, she would miss a great deal: her friends, her summer, and most of all her soccer games.

Something had to happen soon. The stewardess was giving them the eye.

Kim decided to try a different approach. "Uncle Piet might send out a search party." Kim peeked across to see if she was getting through. "What about setting up your e-mail and reporting to your radio station?" She spit out every thought that flitted into her head. "What about Grandpa, the farm, the cousins?" she added.

Had Riana heard her? She had heard all right. Riana pushed her smooth blonde hair back from her face to reveal trapped-animal eyes. "He won't come," she whispered.

"Who?" asked Kim.

Riana's eyes contracted into an icy stare. "Your grandfather."

Kim decided to go easy. She was relieved to see that her mother was at least making an effort to put her book and glasses into her cloth slingbag. "Mom, remember the Cape of Good Hope?" Kim said gently. "Warm Indian Ocean on one side, cold Atlantic on the other? You promised to show me not one ocean, but two."

It worked! At the word *ocean*, Riana's eyes lit up. "Cape Town is the most beautiful city in the world," she said, as she fished out their passports.

In the terminal building a sandy-haired man waved fervently at them. "There's your uncle," pointed Riana. Uncle Piet had short hair parted at the side, glasses, and a flushed, choirboy look. He wore a tracksuit and running shoes, and on his head was a lopsided Canadian baseball cap that slid even more lopsidedly as he squeezed Riana. By the time he got to Kim, the cap was dangerously close to his eyes. "I'm your *Oom* Piet," he said, pounding Kim on the back as he embraced her.

*Great*, thought Kim. His breath was a mixture of tobacco and peppermints.

"Good flight?" He drew back and looked her over. Kim knew what he would see: a tall, thirteen-year-old girl with a frizzy mess of hair, because she had been too tired to brush it. What he couldn't see was how weird it felt to be here. Canada was the only home she'd ever known. And yet she had no relatives there. Uncle Piet was the first family member she had ever set eyes on.

"It was okay, Ooo Piet," she said taking a quick step back.

"*Oom* Piet," Riana corrected, smiling tightly at her brother.

"She's going to be very tall," he told Riana.

Kim didn't like the way her uncle studied her from head to toe. But she liked it when he added, "She's not got your physique."

"Thank goodness," said Riana, raking her fingers through her hair. Oom Piet had the same blond hair as Riana. Like her mom's, Piet's hair could be tamed with a moist comb. In total contrast, Kim's brown mop was so thick and fly-away, she could only control it with an extra wide elastic band, the kind that fastened hefty vegetables together in supermarkets.

Half an hour later, they were strapped into Piet's Land Rover. It was a big vehicle, but Kim felt crowded by the luggage wedged at her feet. Plus, she shared her seat with an angular, sharp-eared dog. His breath smelled like fish and his hair was tangled with things from the bush. He used his large, yellow, pre-historic toenails to get at the twigs and insects that were living in his fur.

"*Bliksem!*" Oom Piet yelled when the dog itched wildly with his back foot.

The 4 X 4 snaked around a cliff-hugging road beside the sea. Cape Town was on the farthest tip of Africa – Afrika, as Kim now thought of it. "What do you think of our Mother City, Kim?" her uncle asked as he steered the car. "I'll take you on a little drive."

Kim squirmed and could not look out the window. The cliff was very steep. One mistake on the winding road and they would plunge headfirst into the sea.

"I guess staying in Africa will make up for all the boring times I had growing up in Calgary." Kim gripped her hands together and spoke to no one in particular. Beside her, Bliksem distracted himself with dog business – itching, drooling, and panting. Riana nodded vaguely, but her eyes did not stray from the ocean.

Piet and Riana chatted together in Afrikaans, the language they had spoken as children. Kim knew it was a mixture of Dutch, German, and other languages, but she did not understand a word of it. Unable to move her legs, she stretched her weary arms and hoped they were not talking about her. As if there wasn't already enough secrecy in her family, she would now have to hear Afrikaans spoken around her, making more secrets, shutting her out. The only word she recognized was *Melkweg*, the name of Riana's family farm. *Melkweg* meant "Milky Way," and Kim knew that the Milky Way Farm was located a long car ride from Cape Town, in the middle of the Karoo, an arid plateau where the night skies are clear and filled with stars.

Kim listened to the strange language with its dry, harsh, scraping sounds. What if this language had been *her* mother tongue instead of English? If her mom had stayed in South Africa and not emigrated when she was pregnant with Kim, they would be living in Africa today and speaking this language as their own.

Suddenly Oom Piet turned sharply from Riana and spoke in English. Had they been arguing? Or did he break into English because he remembered that Kim was alive and well and sitting in the backseat?

"You must be careful," Oom Piet told Riana. "You will make enemies."

Riana turned her nose up at this and said, "Piet, I think I know what I'm getting into."

"The Truth Commission is not accepted by everyone," Piet responded. "Some see it as a witch hunt designed to stir up hatred."

When they were deciding to come to South Africa, Kim's mother had explained to her that the Truth and Reconciliation Commission was controversial. Some people supported it and others did not. It was set up by the new government. The commission's job was to look at the injustices caused by the old system which had forcibly segregated the races of South Africa into Blacks, Whites, Indians, and Coloreds. But this was the first time that Kim realized that covering the commission might be risky for the journalists.

Riana appeared to ignore Oom Piet's warning. Instead, she stared out the window at the sea and said, "Pull over, please."

Oom Piet steered his Land Rover to a lookout point high above the ocean. As soon as the car stopped, Riana bolted out and kicked off her shoes. Kim could not believe her eyes. She watched her mother whistle for Bliksem to join her, and the two of them darted toward the cliff edge. The sun was setting and Oom Piet suggested Kim watch the fiery colors from where she sat. In fact, her uncle wedged his arm across the backseat, between Kim and the car door, making her a prisoner there.

"Give your ma a moment alone," he commanded. "She's finally home."

*Is he crazy?* thought Kim. Home is Canada! Kim was exhausted from the two punishing flights, and her lips and throat were as parched as sand. What was her mother doing, standing there in bare feet, her fingers dangling behind the ears of a strange mutt? Was this the same mother who did not allow a single pet to share their Calgary house? And who did Piet think he was, fencing her in with his arm? His baseball cap had seen better days and, like Riana, he threw any old piece of clothing on his body. Now he took out his cigarette pack, and without asking Kim if she minded, lit a cigarette.

Kim circled her tongue frantically around her mouth trying to locate one tiny glob of moisture. She hoped she wasn't getting sick. Her uncle's cigarette sucked all the air out of the Land Rover.

Riana was taking a long time. Putting her chocolate-smeared fingers to her cheeks as if to cool herself, Kim spoke hurriedly: "Did you know my dad?"

The question slid out as quickly as a snake's tongue. She had had no intention of asking Oom Piet about her father, but she had done it, almost against her own will.

"My father," she repeated. "Did you know him?"

Oom Piet avoided looking at her by taking off his glasses and polishing them on his sweatshirt. She had caught him off guard, all right, and Kim knew that catching people off guard was the only way to get answers from them. If only he would give her some detail. But instead of responding to her question, he plunked his glasses back on his nose and gestured away from the sea toward the darkness on the other side of the road. "Look. Behind that cliff is our famous Table Mountain. Not a speck of snow on it. Not like your Rockies, hey."

Kim dug her fingers into the car seat in frustration. It was too late. Her mother and Bliksem were strolling back to the car. The discussion of her father was dead. For now.

"You'll see a better view of it from the cottage," added her uncle. "Some days clouds form like a tablecloth over its top. They say you can read the weather by it."

Bliksem leaped into the backseat, swishing his dragon tail this way and that until he got comfortable. "I'm dying of thirst," Kim said as her mom climbed into the front seat.

"Darling, you had some juice on the plane," Riana mumbled, her mind obviously still on the ocean.

"My girl," said Oom Piet, his cigarette between his lips. "Would you like a peppermint?"

"No," Kim mumbled and pressed herself into the seat. The warm fish-breeze of Bliksem's breath made Kim blink. "No, thank you," she added grimly.

Oom Piet pulled his vehicle back onto the road. "We're almost there," he said. "The cottage is small, but cozy. It's Victorian. Over a hundred years old."

Kim glared at the back of her mother's head. It drove her crazy that Riana would not talk to her about her father. The only detail Riana had revealed was this: he was South African too. As if Kim hadn't put two and two together! Then, the day after Riana had accepted this assignment, she presented Kim with a flimsy notebook that had belonged to her father. "This is the last thing he ever gave me," Riana had said. "He wanted to be a writer."

Kim couldn't wait to be alone with the notebook. A few minutes later she was sitting by the lamp in her bedroom, leafing through the scribble. Guess what! The notebook was illegible – written in a language she could not decipher. Eventually, Kim gave up, placed the notebook under her mattress, and tried to forget about it. Yet when she packed for the three-month trip to Africa, Kim put the notebook in her carry-on luggage, not allowing it to be away from her in the belly of the plane.

Riana glanced at Kim through the rearview mirror and then dreamily gazed out the window.

"Where is my father?" Kim mumbled. She mouthed the words into the soft place between her fingers where she could smell the chocolate from the airplane. Of course, no one heard her.

# TWO

# THE COTTAGE AND THE SHACK

Outside Kim and Riana's cottage, plant creepers and fig-leaf fingers shimmered in the moonlight. Beside the front door, which Oom Piet unlocked, stood a high white trellis, at the bottom of which were the cut-off wooden stalks of roses.

"Hey, it's dark," said Kim, shivering.

"Those Victorians knew something all right," Oom Piet said, as they stepped inside. "Small windows hold the warmth in winter and shut out the hot sun in summer."

The house was not very big, but the rooms felt spacious because of the high ceilings. The cottage had a roof made of tin and the walls were thick and cream-colored. It reminded Kim of a gingerbread house. In the main room the shelves sagged with the weight of books and shells and carvings of zebras and giraffes. At one end of the room was a cast-iron fireplace with a rectangular chimney. Behind the screen, a fire was burning.

"So, you like it?" asked Piet. The skin around his eyes crinkled when he smiled.

"Yes," said Kim. A deep sense of relief filled her. After so many hours to get here, and her mother's unnerving reluctance when the plane landed, the small house was the most wonderful thing she had ever seen.

"We rescued this cottage from ruin about twelve years ago," he said. "We usually rent it to tourists. But it's winter. You still thirsty?"

"Yes," said Kim as she left the fireplace and followed her uncle through the swinging door that separated the kitchen from the living room.

"How about that?" said Piet, opening the fridge. "Guava juice." He handed Kim a Tetra Pak.

"Buy a donkey," answered Kim. *Baie dankie* was "thank you very much" in Afrikaans, one of the few expressions she had mastered as a child.

Piet and Riana exchanged smiles as Kim sucked up the thick, unfamiliar juice. Then Riana unloaded her coat, purse, and the contents of her sling bag onto the middle of the wobbly, wooden kitchen table.

"The cottage is perfect," said Kim and her mother at the same time. Amazing. They both agreed, for once.

Oom Piet looked relieved. "The garden is huge," he said. "For a large part of the year there are lemons on that tree and the wild fennel grows as high as your head."

Kim moved to the back of the kitchen. Piet showed her how the garden door opened – in half, upper and lower – like a stable door. Then he unlocked a set of burglar bars outside it. In the garden ferns and fig trees glistened in the moonlight and shivered all the way back to the neighbor's wall. Kim blinked her tired eyes. They were playing tricks on her. She thought she saw a flat-roofed shack in the far corner of the yard.

Oom Piet took a gum packet out of his pocket and, after offering some to Kim and Riana, folded a stick into his mouth. "When must I tell Pa you'll be coming to the farm?" he asked, relocking the bars.

"I don't know," Riana said quickly. She had refused the gum and was shifting through her stuff on the table.

Chewing, Uncle Piet said, "I could fetch you and Kim next weekend."

Riana looked tense. This was definitely not a conversation she wanted to have, but Piet pushed on. "Come now, Riana," he said. "There's always the weekend following."

Riana inhaled sharply. "No, Piet, I have to work." Oom Piet chewed in silence, then fumbled for his cigarettes, but thankfully did not take one out. Kim continued to stare out into the yard. Not only was there a shack at the bottom of the garden, but a light flickered inside it – an unsteady light like that of a candle. The shadow of a figure moved past the window. "Who's that?" Kim asked.

"That's Lettie," her uncle said. He turned to Riana. "You remember Lettie from the farm. When I bought this cottage I asked her to move down to take care of it. She agreed. She said her children could get a better education in Cape Town."

Riana's mouth opened and her eyes lit up. "Lettie Bandla?" she gasped.

Uncle Piet nodded. "*Ja*. Her boy is around Kim's age. He stays with her on school nights. Must I ask her to come up to make tea?"

He went to exit the back door, but Riana's words froze him in his tracks. Her pleasure at hearing Lettie's name had totally disappeared. "No, I can't!" she snapped. "I don't want a maid."

Kim's uncle was surprised at Riana's mood change. "Riana, you are tired," he reasoned. "Let's have some tea."

"Rubbish! I am not tired," her mother shouted. "This is why I left South Africa. This is why I had to get away. You never understood how much I hated it all!"

"Calm down, woman." Piet's face was red. He jammed another gum stick into his mouth. "Where in the world are there no haves and have-nots? So, you don't have poor in Canada?"

Kim chewed on her straw. Since Oom Piet had opened the half-door a wild, damp, midnight smell filled the kitchen.

"You used to be very fond of Lettie," her uncle said. "What must I do? She comes with the house."

Riana pressed her lips together. "You make it sound like she's a piece of furniture."

Uncle Piet snorted, "*Ag* man, stop. She relies on this job. She takes care of the renters."

Suddenly he turned and looked at Kim. "I'll show you to your bedroom," he said, picking up her suitcase and motioning for her to follow. Kim wanted to hear more of what they were saying, but reluctantly she followed Oom Piet out of the kitchen, through the living room, and down the hall. The floor seemed to sway under her feet. How many hours – days even – had it been since she had put her head down on a bed?

Piet opened a door and set her suitcase inside it. "My girl, keep the burglar bars locked across your window," he instructed her. Then he left the room and closed the door behind him.

Kim heard the low rumble of voices. Riana and Oom Piet were now speaking Afrikaans, but Kim could predict the conversation. She knew her mother hated master-servant, as she called it. It was the way she summed up her old life in South Africa.

Kim herself didn't know how she felt about the fact that a boy and his mother were living in their yard. She was reeling with fatigue and not able to make sense of it. Her throat was burning and she was sure she was getting sick. She inspected the room that would be her home for the next three months.

The first thing she saw were bunk beds with leopard print bedspreads. All her life Kim had dreamed about having bunk beds. She had begged her mother to buy them rather than the prissy white-and-gold girl's bed she acquired when her mother got a promotion last year. "What were you thinking?" Kim had demanded when her mother began to spread the frilly pink bedspread on the new bed the very day after her promotion. "Sugar and spice and everything nice," she had sung sarcastically.

"Do you mind?" Riana asked as her goofy, gaudy glasses slid down her nose.

"What about bunk beds?" Kim had demanded.

"You do not have a sister so bunk beds are impractical." Case closed.

The reality was, Kim loved the idea of a sister as much as she loved the idea of bunk beds. Someone to gab with late at night. Someone to pillow fight into submission each morning. Someone to share feelings and secrets with. Her mother had never come right out and said it, but Kim knew that

Riana had no intention of marrying or having any more babies.

On the wall beside the beds hung a square mirror with a border of polished stones. Kim barely recognized herself. Her tired eyes were sunk into her skull like dark pools of tar. Whose eyes were those? Certainly not her mom's watery blue eyes.

"Can I at least see a photo?" she had once asked her mother. "You must have packed one photo of him."

"I left South Africa in a hurry," Riana told her. It was just like Riana not to have taken the right things with her.

Below the mirror, in the middle of a small table, were half a dozen short-stemmed flowers in a glass jar. A ribbon was wrapped and carefully tied around the belly of the jar. She wondered: Had the woman in the garden started the fire in the fireplace and left the flowers?

Kim unpacked her carry-on. At the bottom of the bag was her father's thin notebook. Taking it with her, she scrambled up the wooden ladder to the top bunk.

Outside, the wind groaned and howled. No doubt whatsoever – a storm was coming. The Cape of Good Hope had the most famous storms in the world. Kim had read about how gale winds and waves ripped huge ships apart and then bashed the cargo and survivors against the rocks. Arrow-carrying herdsmen and night animals met anyone who was "lucky" enough to reach the shore alive.

Suddenly she heard a noise out in the garden. She edged over and leaned closer to the window. She could see the shack clearly from this angle. It was hardly bigger than a garden shed and was painted white with a wooden door that swung out in two pieces. The top half was open and a tall boy stood in the doorway. In the darkness she could barely make out his features, but he appeared to be looking up at the house. A moment later he moved farther back into the room.

Kim wrapped the leopard print bedspread around herself. Her eyes were so heavy she could barely keep them open. The voices in the other room had died down. Her uncle, who had left Bliksem alone in the Land Rover, would have to return soon to the farm.

Kim placed her pillow at the small of her back and collapsed into it, her father's notebook on her lap. She blinked her tired eyes trying to focus on the lettering that was on the inside of the back cover. She angled the notebook so it caught the light from the moon. There it was. *Afrika, Afrika, Afrika* was scribbled over and over.

Her spirits lifted. All these years her mother could keep secrets because they were in Canada – where no one knew their story, where there were no relatives, no one to question anything. But that was no longer the case.

She shivered and pulled the leopard cloth tighter around her shoulders. She was now in the same country, likely the same city as her father. She had never been this close to him. Surely it was only a matter of time before they would meet.

# THREE

# SCHOOL

**S**ure enough, the next morning Kim woke up with a throat as sore as when she was a little girl with tonsillitis. Riana told her to stay in the top bunk and sleep while she researched stories to send back to the News Director at her radio station. But Riana had trouble coping with Kim's cold and the demands of the new job. Before the morning was finished, and despite the fact that she had declared numerous times that she would not be a white madam with a maid, Riana rushed into the garden to enlist Lettie's help.

Kim heard them approach. "Kim, this is Lettie," said Riana. Kim turned her throbbing head to see a stout black woman moving toward her bed.

Lettie wore a navy beret and navy sweater over a white uniform. She stood beside the bunk bed and peered up at Kim for a long time. "Shame, you must drink," she said as she raised an eyebrow. Lettie wore slippers and they made flip-flop noises as she crossed the wooden floor. "You better drink right now."

"Fine," moaned Kim as she rolled her head from one side of the pillow to the other.

Lettie set to work. She made bowls of sweetened tea and placed them near Kim's bed. Kim slurped the syrupy tea, dark as the earth, and made the best of her illness. She was in no hurry to leave her top bunk. As far as she was concerned, it was summer, and she should not be in school at all. Kim was going to have that argument again with Riana as soon as she felt better.

For two days Riana was gone most of the time and Lettie cared for Kim. When Kim felt better, she propped herself up in bed and Lettie sat in the chair by the window with crochet wool and a silver hook in her hands.

"So, when will you get up for school?" Lettie asked, as she moved her heavy body in the chair. "Tomorrow?"

"Nope," said Kim. "I'm not going to school."

"Aai, aai, Kim, you must not hate school."

"I don't hate school, but I'm sick."

"So, then, should we say a prayer?" Lettie asked.

"It's okay," said Kim. "But thanks, anyway."

Lettie explained that she was now a believing Xhosa woman. She no longer believed in witch doctors, or *tokoloshes*, but in the words of her minister.

"What's a tokolo-e?" asked Kim.

"Tok – o – loshe," Lettie said the word slowly. "He has a hairy body and a baboon-like face and hides under the bed at night." Lettie told Kim that when she was a child, many African women she knew in rural areas slept with their beds on high bricks to avoid these dwarf-like wizards. "My two children convinced me to stop fearing tokoloshes or taking herbal potions from the *sangoma* – witch doctor." Lettie laughed. "I'm now a modern mama."

"Where is your son?" Kim asked. "Why doesn't he come inside?"

"He's not here today. He stays in the township with his sister and grandfather on weekends. Nearby where the soccer field is located. They don't have permission to play on that field but men and boys do so anyway," she added as she raised her eyebrows.

It was impossible for Kim to judge Lettie's age. She seemed older than Riana. Lettie was slow and capable like a grandmother, whereas Riana was quick and active like a teenager. Lettie was very neat and Riana was quite a slob. Lettie's smile warmed the room while Riana's anxiety could freeze the air around you in seconds. Kim could have stayed at home forever with Lettie, but two mornings later, Riana called the new school and told them to expect Kim.

"Not fair. This is my summer holiday," argued Kim. To Kim's horror, Riana produced a new school uniform, a green skirt and blazer along with a stiff yellow blouse, and made her put it on. In Canada, she wore what she liked to school.

"Think of what an enriching experience it will be to go to a foreign school," Riana said, as they climbed into the car that Oom Piet had arranged for them.

Before Kim knew it they were in front of the iron gates of the school. "I'm still sick," said Kim. "I'm really not much better."

"You are," stated Riana. "And I'm late for work."

Whenever Riana went out to work, she replaced her cloth slingbag with a battered old brown-red leather bag. Now it was sprawled open on the seat beside Kim. It smelled of smoke-filled rooms and Riana's tangy musk. Whenever Kim tried to point out the slick new briefcases in stylish store windows, her mother would say, "I like this old thing. It's me."

"If I'm not here after school then Lettie will fetch you," Riana said, getting out of the car.

Kim pulled a face. "I can walk home," she insisted. "I have a key."

"It's not safe, darling. Seriously. Lettie will fetch you."

"Lettie doesn't drive."

"She will come for you on foot," Riana said as her cell phone sang its silly jingle.

"I thought you didn't want to be a white madam with a maid," Kim said. "I thought you had principles about it."

Riana sighed and jammed the phone to her ear. Kim remained in the car and fumbled in her blazer pocket for her Smarties. She gobbled them down. What amazed Kim was this: back home, her disorganized, untidy mother never had a nanny or a cleaning lady, much less a full-time maid. After recovering from the initial shock of seeing Lettie, Riana appeared to enjoy giving her instructions on what to cook, how to wash something, and when to pick up Kim. Even though they appeared friendly, at the same time, Kim noticed a distance between them. "White madame with a maid" was a side of her mother that Kim had never witnessed before.

The phone call ended. "I have to leave," Riana said, as she flagged down a teacher who happened to be passing. "Sorry. It's my daughter's first day. Could you show her to the office?" she asked the gray-haired teacher.

"Of course," the woman said as she gave Riana a thorough once-over. "Come now. The bell will ring soon."

Reluctantly, Kim got out of the car. Kim knew what the teacher was seeing. Riana wore a frayed man's shirt and striped pants that tied at the ankles. Just before the car spun off, Kim resisted the urge to tell her mother that she couldn't go off dressed like that.

Kim followed the teacher beside a green manicured lawn. The school was surrounded by thick, whitewashed walls and iron railings. Ivy swirled around two thick pillars that flanked the entrance. Kim, uncomfortable in her unfamiliar school uniform, despised wearing a skirt, but she did enjoy wearing a tie.

"What school are you transferring from?" the teacher asked, looking Kim over. Her accent was clipped and formal, different from Oom Piet's.

"I'm from Canada." When she spoke her mouth was thick with chocolate.

"Canada?" The teacher's gray brows lifted. "Why are you in South Africa?"

"My mother is a journalist," Kim explained. "She's covering the Truth and Reconciliation Commission." The teacher stared back from behind her glasses.

They arrived at the main office as the bell rang. The teacher tried to determine where Kim belonged. Two secretaries were chatting about a mid-day burglary in one of their apartments.

"No, really, they took everything. Even the milk in the fridge," said the brunette.

"Jeez," her blonde friend replied. "What are you going to do?"

"Get a watchdog, man."

"Or a gun. I got one."

"Or both. I mean it."

They finally tore themselves away to come to Kim's end of the counter. No students were left in the hall. No doubt whatsoever, Kim would be brought in late and all eyes would be glued on her.

"Room 20," announced the blonde secretary. "Miss Phillips' class." She had fragile, almost blue-white skin and Kim had trouble imagining her carrying a gun around, let alone shooting it.

The teacher led Kim down the empty hall and knocked on the first door to the right. "Prudy, this is Kim van der Merwe," she said, when Miss Phillips opened the door. "She's Canadian. Apparently her mother is here to cover the TRC."

Both women exchanged a look. It was impossible for Kim to figure out what the glance meant. She remembered how her uncle had warned them that some people did not support the commission and suddenly, Kim was sure that Miss Phillips disapproved of the commission and of her too. She wished she could turn around and escape. Her throat was still scratchy and she still had a cough. She longed for the peace of her top bunk bed.

Kim was shown to a desk halfway to the back. She sat down, opened her pencil case, and took out a pencil. Miss Phillips was still observing her. And so was everyone else. Kim rubbed the back of her hand across her mouth, hoping there were no traces of chocolate there.

Kim peeled off her blazer and placed it on the seat beside her. As she did she turned and peered right into the almond-shaped eyes of a girl sitting behind her. The girl smiled politely. On the other side of Kim, three or four black students sat together. While Miss Phillips wrote on the board, Kim listened as they spoke softly in their language. Every once in a while an English word or phrase would stand out crystal clear. It was odd to hear familiar words bounce around in the middle of foreign sentences.

Then the worse thing that could happen happened. Instead of starting the lesson, Miss Phillips put down her piece of chalk and directed her eyes so they were drilling right through Kim.

"This is Kim van der Merwe," she said as everyone turned to stare again. "Kim will be with us for three months. Her mother has come all the way from Canada to cover the Truth and Reconciliation Commission." The teacher paused in front of Kim's desk. Kim's heart stopped for a second. What if Miss Phillips asked her a question that she couldn't answer?

Miss Phillips moved on and addressed the entire classroom. "An historical event is happening at this moment in our country. Who can explain what this commission is about?"

No one wanted to answer. Unfazed, Miss Phillips leaned forward and said: "We all understand what the word *truth* means. What does the word *reconciliation* mean?"

A dark-skinned boy near the front of the room shot up his hand. "Reconciliation means to forgive," he answered and then gave himself a hero's smile. Kim knew the type.

"That's right, Jerry," said Miss Phillips. "Do you understand why this commission was started and how it works?"

"It's about healing the past," he fired back. "Before we can build a new country, we must look at the wrongs of apartheid."

*Apartheid.* It sounded different with his accent, but Kim knew the word. She remembered when she was much younger, perhaps five or six, Riana had first told her about it. "How does it work?" Kim had asked noticing the little word *apart* tucked into the larger word. "It means totally separating black and white people," said Riana. "It means forbidding black people to swim in the same swimming pools as white people." She went on to explain that a black nanny could go to the pool or the beach to look after a white child, but the nanny was not allowed in the water. "What if she went into the water?" Kim had asked. "It was against the law," Riana replied. "She would get into serious trouble." Even at a young age, Kim had been shocked by this injustice.

Kim noticed that Miss Phillips was smiling at Jerry. He spoke as if he had memorized the answer from a book. It was the sort of answer that teachers like, and Miss Phillips was no exception.

"Thank you, Jerry," she said. "Many people will come forward to tell their stories to the commission. Some of the people will be victims. Others will be perpetrators – those who carried out the wrongdoings. The commission will listen to all the people and check out all the stories."

Kim scribbled in her notebook. The heat was off and she began to relax. Miss Phillips had called the commission historical. Suddenly Kim was proud of her mother.

A white boy across the room waved his hand. Alarmed, Kim glanced in his direction. His ears flapped open instead of lying flat against his skull.

"Yes, James," Miss Phillips nodded.

James leaped to his feet. His jacket was draped over his shoulders and it swamped his short frame. "My dad says this commission is a waste of time. He says they should just get on with building a new country and not drag up the past and waste tax

payers' money doing so." His large ears had become
flushed with the effort it took to speak in public. He
looked right at Kim and added, "My dad says that
the foreign press uses our troubles for entertainment."

James sat down. Kim stared down at her paper.
Would Miss Phillips ask her to defend her mother in
front of the entire classroom?

A tall black boy beside Kim put up his hand.
He got to his feet to speak. "In 1990 my pa was
taken away in the middle of the night in the back of
a police van. We searched for months but never
found him. My mother knows that the commission
will not bring my father back, but maybe our questions will be answered."

Kim looked at the boy. He had a distinct
African accent, yet he spoke clearly. As he sat down,
he noticed Kim staring at him. He returned the
look, but his eyes were impossible to read. Were
they cold or curious? Then Kim noticed the cover
of his exercise book. On it he had scribbled *Afrika*
over and over.

"Thank you, Themba," Miss Phillips said as she
began to hand out the assignment for the day.

At the break Kim gravitated toward the field
where a few boys were kicking a soccer ball around.
Soccer had been her favorite sport at home. She
played on a girl's team that competed all over
western Canada. With longing she watched Themba

pass the ball between himself and another black boy. A white boy stood farther down the field at the goal. She couldn't believe the black kids were still talking about the Truth Commission.

"It's rubbish," said Themba to the other boy. As he spoke he kicked his toe into the dirt field. "Reconciliation means that killers can walk free."

"President Mandela has shown forgiveness," the other black boy argued. "Why can't you? You are what – better than Mandela?"

Themba kicked the ball hard. The white boy lunged for it, but the ball rebounded off a goalpost toward Kim. She blocked the ball with her body and kicked it straight back to Themba.

"Can I play too?" she asked.

"A girl play soccer?" laughed the shorter boy. "Are you mad?"

"Shut up, Sipho," Themba said. He kicked the ball in Kim's direction. "Let her play," he shouted.

Relieved and happy to be included, Kim ran up the field with the ball between her feet. Themba was a good sprinter, but she swirled to one side, took the ball, and lost him. Then she jerked left and right past Sipho and charged up to the goalpost.

Kim took her time setting up the shot. She was wide open, but she needed to kick the ball with force and control. She heard her Calgary coach yelling in her ear. *Slow down! Be precise!* She aimed for the far

corner of the goal and belted it. The white boy fell
to his stomach but missed the ball. She scored!

"Hey," said Themba coming up behind her. His
dark eyes, set deep in his nut-brown face, were
encouraging. But a mocking grin spread across his
face. He picked up a twig from the ground and held
it near her mouth as if the twig was a microphone.
Then he changed his voice, making it deep and
urgent, like a sportscaster. "Miss Kim, tell our
viewers how it feels to play on a real soccer team."

Kim took a step back. "How did you know
that?"

He moved the imaginary microphone from
her mouth to his. "Does the name Lettie Bandla
ring a bell?" he asked, planting one hand on his hip.

"What about her?" Kim asked. He couldn't
possibly know about Lettie or the blue and maroon
soccer uniform she had brought with her to South
Africa.

He looked her straight in the eye. "Surprise!"
he said. "My ma and I live at the bottom of your
garden."

# FOUR

# THEMBA

**K**im couldn't wait for her first day at the new school to be over. Through the long afternoon she was conscious of Themba who sat silently in the desk across from her. She didn't know what to make of him. Themba had obviously enjoyed her shock over finding out that he was living in her garden. The whole situation was weird: this country, this boy in a shack in her yard, this school. She decided to act as if none of these unusual things really affected her. She wasn't afraid of Themba. She would act as if he were any boy she knew back home. Her opportunity came a few moments later when Miss Phillips left the classroom to speak to someone in the hall. Almost at once the students began to talk amongst themselves. Kim turned to Themba, as casually as she could manage, and asked him why he spelled Africa with a *K*.

"Oh that," Themba responded giving Kim a look she couldn't figure out. "It's my poor Bantu education. I'm afraid we natives can't spell."

For a moment there was silence as Kim wondered if he was angry.

"It's a joke, hey, Kim," he finally said. Then his mouth spread into a wide grin — the first real smile Kim had seen from him.

She made a mental note to get back at him. Somehow.

"Don't you have jokes in Canada?" he added with a wink. When he winked he reminded Kim of Lettie. He had the same teasing eyes as his mother's, glossy as black river stones.

"No, we don't," Kim fired back. "It's illegal. They put you in jail."

Themba pointed at a framed poster that hung beside the blackboard. "Look at the first line of our new anthem. *Nkosi Sikelel' iAfrika*," he said, as he read the words out loud for her. "God bless Africa."

Kim almost told Themba about the map she'd drawn on the plane, and how she had scribbled Afrika over and over not really knowing why. But she didn't trust him enough to tell him anything about herself. Instead she said, "How come I didn't see you yesterday or the day before?"

"On weekends I stay in the township outside Cape Town," he answered.

"Alone?"

He smiled at her question. "I stay with my sister and grandfather."

"Why don't you go to a school out there?"

Themba's smile disappeared and his color deepened. "Guys are knifed to death over bags of marbles. Girls are raped on the way to gym class. Township schools are shit."

Kim stiffened. At that moment Miss Phillips returned and the classroom quieted down. Kim was greatly relieved, for she had no idea how to respond to Themba.

There was a great deal she did not understand about South Africa and the four days she had spent sick in bed had not made things any clearer. This world belonged to Themba and Lettie, to her mother and Oom Piet, but not to her. She had no business at all in Africa, and that morning, on the way to school, she had told Riana so. "Living here will make you appreciate Canada more," her mother had said.

After school, Kim grabbed her jacket and bag and went quickly to the front gate to see if her mother had come. Riana was nowhere to be seen, and Kim decided that she would walk the short distance home. She had memorized the route between the cottage and the school. By foot it would take fifteen, twenty minutes at the most. She would stick to the busy street that went up the mountain. She could see the street from the school parking lot. She knew for sure that it eventually intersected her street.

Kim looked up at the mountain. Just as Oom Piet had promised, clouds were racing to form a tablecloth on its unusual flat top. It reassured her to see Table Mountain. Because of its constant presence above the city, she could not easily lose her way.

Yet, as she crossed the intersection, Kim hesitated. How many times had her mother warned her? "You are not in Canada." "Don't leave the yard." "If you are alone, the streets are out of bounds." Whenever Riana ventured out, and with a meticulousness she never had back home, she checked the windows, and carefully locked the doors and security gates. Once in the car, Riana immediately rolled up each window and locked each door. Last night, when Kim had felt better, they went out after dark to rent a video. Kim was shocked to see that her mother slowed down at a red light, but after carefully checking from left to right, continued on before the light changed to green. Her mother would never go through a red light in Canada. Riana explained that gangs hijacked cars at red lights and it made no difference if windows were up or doors were locked.

Kim knew without a doubt that her mother would be angry if she left the school and walked home alone. But Riana was working late and would never know. Kim fingered the key in her pocket. It was a bright sunny afternoon. No big deal. She would walk faster than usual and be home in twelve minutes. The light changed and Kim crossed the street.

On the pavement directly ahead of her was a group of street hawkers. Some sold vegetables; others stood by a trolley of old clothes and passed a bottle between them. The men chatted together in their language, but as she approached, they stopped talking and stared at her. One looked directly at her watch. Panic gripped her. She froze.

"Where are you going?" Themba yelled as he sprinted up to her side. He pointed across the street. "Ma is frantic."

Kim turned and saw Lettie and another black woman near the school parking lot. Lettie was striding up the hill and she was obviously angry.

"What's the problem?" Kim asked.

Themba scrunched up his face. "My ma is mad at me that you ran off like that. She made me promise to protect you like a little rare bird in a cage."

"That's ridiculous."

At that moment Lettie, out of breath, reached them. "Kim, you can't walk home alone," she told her between gulps of air. "You must wait for us." As soon as she was able, she introduced Kim to the other woman. "Ntombi is my sister-in-law."

Ntombi was slim and attractive and, unlike Lettie, she wore nothing on her head so her many tight braids hung loose. She gave Kim the once-over, then turned to Lettie. "Hey, she's not so tall. She is not as tall as you make her out to be."

"Why would I exaggerate?" Lettie and her sister-in-law broke into a nervous laugh and a look of relief passed between them. Kim felt badly that she had worried them. "Ntombi and I will walk you home," Lettie said. "We will go first to the dry cleaners to fetch your mom's blazer."

In her sick bed Kim had heard the story from Lettie of her young sister-in-law, Ntombi, who was twenty-five years younger than Lettie. Ntombi refused to spend the rest of her life in a township slum. Since apartheid had ended, and she could live anywhere she wanted, she was looking for a room somewhere in town. According to Lettie, she enjoyed clubbing and pubbing on the waterfront of Cape Town. "Not a day passes where I don't fear for her future," Lettie had said more than once.

Themba shifted his weight from side to side. His face lit up. "Ma, go home and rest," he said. "Let Ntombi come with us. We'll fetch the blazer and then take the bus straight back to Kim's house."

Ntombi rubbed her fingertips through Themba's tight hair and smiled mischievously at Kim. "Quick, give me the laundry ticket," she said. "I have to be somewhere else now-now." Kim liked the warmth in Ntombi's face and she could tell that Themba's young aunt would be less strict with them.

"Okay, off you go," said Lettie nodding at Ntombi. She turned in the direction of the mountain and slowly walked away.

On the way to the dry cleaners, Kim, Themba, and Ntombi strolled through the Botanical Gardens. It was filled with exotic trees, impressive fountains, and large cages of birds. Themba wanted to show Kim the gray squirrels, which were supposed to have been brought from North America in the first place.

"How did you get to be such a world expert on squirrels?" Kim asked. She was used to boys being shorter than she was. Not Themba – he was tall.

"I read all about them," he said.

An old bearded man on a bench waved. He was dressed in a worn sports jacket and trousers, but he had no shoelaces in his boots. He held his hat in his hands. "Excuse me, does you have two rands for a cup of coffee?"

"Sorry my chappie," Themba answered as he fished out a coin and gave it to him. "I have only one coin."

Ntombi clicked her tongue against the inside of her cheek. "No man, Themba," she scowled as they walked away. "That *bergie* might have a knife."

In silence they continued down a tree-lined lane. "Speaking of criminals," Themba said, "I want to show Kim something." He led them toward a large old-fashioned building in the center of the gardens. "The museum is free on Wednesdays."

"*Sies*, Themba," Ntombi said, pulling a face as they mounted the stairs in front of the entrance. "I don't want to see stuffed animals."

"You don't have to come in," Themba replied. "Meet you in the museum shop. Check out the eau de cologne," he teased her. "For you, madam, twenty rands."

Ntombi smiled at him and waved them off.

"I want you to see this," Themba said, as he led Kim into a large room with cases of stuffed animals. His jovial mood was gone. "I want you to see all the things the white settlers put in here," he added. "Cheetahs. Hyenas. Wildebeest." He stared back at her. "Aren't you going to ask me what tribe I come from?"

They were standing in front of a display of beaded headdresses and ornaments. He was testing her, she could tell, but she didn't want him to know she couldn't answer his question. "Tell me then," Kim said, meeting his eyes, "since you're dying to."

"I'm Xhosa," Themba said. He made a clicking noise at the beginning of the word: "X!o-sa," he repeated.

Kim tried to imitate the click with no success.

"Jab your tongue behind your teeth and try."

She did as he said. The sound still came out like a hard *C* and not a click.

Themba shook his head. Now he was smiling, at least. She thought it was a genuine smile, but she was wary too. This friendship wasn't going to be easy. For one thing, she resented the notion that Themba was supposed to watch out for her.

"Look. This is what I wanted you to see," he said.

He led Kim across the room. Kim started. A thin, almost naked person – shorter than Kim – stood behind a large glass case. His almond-shaped eyes looked right at her.

"He's a Bushman," Themba said facing the glass. "A San."

Kim swallowed, trying to recover her wits. For a moment no one spoke. The Bushman's skin was yellow and wrinkled and it looked very real.

"Do they live near Cape Town?" Kim asked.

"They're almost all dead now."

Kim took a step back and realized that the room was filled with large glass display cases. Inside each case, in front of a desert-like background, San men and women were depicted hunting and cooking and going about their daily lives. It was Themba who broke the silence. "At least the Boer

didn't catch us, stuff us in a glass case, and put us in
a museum devoted to animals. Your mom's a Boer,
isn't she?"

Kim wheeled around: "Afrikaner, you mean."

"We call them Boer," Themba said with steely
determination. His eyes narrowed as he added: "We
lived on this continent for centuries before the Boers
and the English came with their armies and laws,
making us the *kaffirs* and them the white bosses."

"What's a kaffir?" she asked.

Themba shot her a look. "Once it was the
word for 'heathen.' Now it's a swearword."

Kim looked down at an ostrich egg used by the
San as a container for water. She could not think of
a single thing to combat Themba's anger. And he was
still talking, "You look nothing like your mother," he
said, taking the conversation in a completely new
direction.

"Actually I was left on a doorstep. There was a
note tucked under my chin and a bottle of Coke in
the bottom of the basket."

She had meant it as a joke, but all the same, Kim
was very irritated. She marched away from Themba
into another room with pottery and large woven
baskets. Who did he think he was? It's true she didn't
look anything like her mom, but why should he
care? "Let's go," she said pointing to the exit.

Outside, they waited for Ntombi on the steps

of the museum. Kim couldn't get the image of the Bushman out of her mind. "I want to go home," she said, shivering.

The awful thing was, she could not go home. Their bungalow in Calgary was two long plane trips away. She was literally on the other side of the world. For a terrifying moment that reality sunk in.

Kim tried to calm herself down. She looked up at the sun above the wide flat mountain to try to judge how late it was. Sunshine made the stone of Table Mountain sparkle as if it had been polished, but the sun would soon set. Her mother had warned her that in Africa the winter sun went down quicker than any place in the world.

She saw Ntombi smoking nearby. Kim was about to run to her and beg that she go back to the cottage where her mom was waiting, when Themba stopped her.

"Kim," he said apologetically, "just forget that, hey."

Kim turned and looked into his eyes. "Just forget I even said that," he added. He paused, as if he wanted to make sure his words sunk in, and then he waved at Ntombi to join them. "I want Kim to see the train station," he said with enthusiasm.

"Train station?" repeated Kim. She felt a rush of excitement. Her love of trains was much bigger than the loneliness she had felt a few seconds earlier.

"Yes, man, Ntombi," Themba said rushing up to his aunt. He danced around Ntombi's thin figure. "*Pleeassssse*," he sang. "Remember the station is beside the dry cleaners and dry cleaners is beside the bus stop."

"Stop it, man, Themba," Ntombi said. She had put out her cigarette and was carefully climbing down the stairs in her platform shoes. "What does Kim want, hey?"

"Let's go, yes," Kim gushed. "I adore trains."

"Okay," Ntombi consented. "A few moments only."

Themba was different from the boys back home. He kept her off-balance, but he also had the ability to make her feel very excited, whether they were playing soccer or having a conversation. No boy had ever made her feel this way. In a flash she forgave him for everything he had said. They practically yanked Ntombi's arm out of its socket as they hurried past the peanut vendors and newspaper boys toward the center of the city.

At the train station Kim and Themba sat on a bench away from the crowd. "You stay put," Ntombi said, as she went to pick up Riana's blazer from a nearby shop.

"We will." Kim and Themba watched a train clatter into the station.

"This platform used to be Whites Only,"

Themba said. "My pa and I would sit on the other side. Afterwards, we'd go together to the shops near the Parade. I remember one time, I must have been five or six, Pa couldn't decide on a particular chicken. He lifted each wing and sniffed under it. When he began to lift the legs, the assistant chased us out of there."

Themba smiled at the memory. Then he shook his head as if to forget it. The noise of the trains vibrated through them.

"I never met my dad," said Kim. "When my mother got pregnant with me, she decided to split South Africa once and for all."

"Did he ever write to you? Ask your ma for a baby picture?"

"No," Kim answered.

"He never tried to ring you?" Themba asked, sitting up very tall on the bench. "Even on your birthday?"

She stiffened. She was surprised by the emotion in Themba's voice. "Why should he?" she asked.

"Because he's your *father*! He should have cared enough to try to find you."

Kim couldn't believe it. What was Themba's problem? His face was flushed and he was shaking. As far as she knew her father had never tried to contact her. He had never attempted to come to Canada to visit.

"Weren't you angry that he never tried to be a father?"

Kim was afraid to speak. She scanned her brain for a joke, but nothing came.

Kim didn't know why her mother kept the secret of her father so tightly sealed. In Canada she had blamed Riana for the silence. But now she was thinking, really it was her father who had not shown the smallest interest in whether Kim was dead or alive. Themba was right. Why had her father not sent one measly letter or asked one single question about her? Out of curiosity if nothing else!

Kim clenched her hands together and bit her lip. Where was Ntombi? Tears, a girl's biggest curse, were threatening to leak out of her eyes. Not for her father – Kim wasn't going to cry for someone she didn't even know! But each of Themba's questions stirred up the loneliness she had felt on the museum steps. She didn't miss her father, not one bit, but she missed her friends, her home, and her own life.

Kim turned her face toward the sound of the train. She would *not* let this foreign boy see her cry.

After a moment, Themba spoke. "I'll help you," he said.

He spoke so quietly that she was not sure she'd heard correctly. She turned to look at him.

"If you want to find your father. I'll help you," he repeated.

# FIVE

# "I CAN'T GET THAT WOMAN'S CRYING OUT OF MY HEAD"

It was two weeks since Kim had left Canada. Time had passed very quickly. The days had turned cold and rainy, and a constant, howling wind made the bare trees scratch and thump across her bedroom window. Often at night, the noise of the branches against the pane jolted Kim awake. For a second, she would forget where she was. Then she would remember how far away she was from her home, and her belly would contract. She'd yank the leopard cloth up to her chin and picture the many ships that had been torn apart while passing the Cape on their way to India.

Kim hadn't seen Themba alone for days. Because of soccer practice, he often stayed nights in his township house. When they spoke last, they had bickered about soccer. Usually he supported her playing soccer, but for some reason he decided to remind her that in his country, in his culture, girls playing soccer were unusual. "Kim! Kim! Don't you understand that girls play field hockey, not soccer?"

As Themba lectured her, the water sloshed
down the windows of the classroom. "What sucker
told you that," Kim had responded. "In Canada we
play hockey on ice, not on grass, and it is played by
both girls and boys."

What was she doing wasting her breath arguing
with Themba? Instead she should be talking to him
about finding her father. Today she was determined
to speak to him alone, but Riana had arranged a
ride home for her with one of the blonde-haired
girls from school. This one was called Marjorie, and
she could already walk straight-spined in a pair of
high heels.

Marjorie found Kim just outside the school.
"There you are," she said. "My mother is waiting in
the car."

"That's all right," Kim said, glancing around
the yard for Themba. She wanted to see if Themba
needed a ride back to the cottage but she couldn't
spot him anywhere. "I can walk," she said.

Marjorie opened the front door of a white
Mercedes Benz. "You cannot," she said. "Mummy,
tell Kim she can't walk home."

"Girls, get in," said Marjorie's mother with half
a smile, half a scowl. She tossed her hair from side to
side with sharp red nails and fumed. "I go mad on
the decor and flowers and some black baboon steals
the car with the wedding dress in the boot."

Black baboon? Kim wondered if she had heard correctly.

Marjorie registered the shock on Kim's face. "Mummy's a wedding planner," she explained to Kim. "She doesn't mean a baboon took the car. She means a man stole it." Marjorie reached back to unlock the door for Kim. "Mummy, that's not nice. You can't say those kinds of things about Blacks now. You could be arrested."

Marjorie and her mom shared a laugh. With disgust Kim flung her canvas knapsack across the leather seat. Two white, spoiled puffs of dogs, who used the backseat as their own private armchair, ran for cover. With a sick feeling, Kim realized that Themba would have been very uncomfortable in the car with them – if he was allowed at all.

They reached Kim's house in all of three minutes. "Thank you," muttered Kim. She grabbed her knapsack by the scruff of its neck, as if it were one of the spoiled dogs, and jumped out. She could have walked home just as quickly. And she hadn't had a chance to talk to Themba.

Entering through the back door of the cottage, Kim kicked off her rubber boots and hung her umbrella on the back railing. She flung her knapsack down on a kitchen chair. Set in the center of the wooden table, on top of a muddled pile of papers and Riana's other work stuff, was a fat chocolate puff and a glass of prune juice – no doubt left for her by Riana.

Kim started when she saw the chocolate puff. In Calgary, no matter how busy or disorganized Riana was, she tried to serve health food to Kim.

Kim saw that the red light of the answering machine was blinking. As she ate the chocolate off the outside of the puff, she pressed the button and Uncle Piet's voice filled the kitchen. It was his second message this week "Riana, listen," he began. "Now I have become this, hey? The go-between for you and Pa. Come on, Bok. The sooner you and Kim come up here the better. Ring me."

Kim shoved the rest of the puff into her mouth, wound the message back, and left it on the machine for her mom. The kitchen door was closed, but Kim could hear Riana and a few of her colleagues talking in the front room. She could smell cigarettes and hear the clink of mugs. This is why Riana had asked Marjorie's mother to collect her from school. Riana was "working" again.

Ignoring the prune juice, Kim cupped her hands under the kitchen tap, and took six or seven swallows of cold water right from the faucet. Then she listened to the conversation in the living room.

"He did that to another human being, then went for drinks afterwards!" It was Riana. Others muttered their disapproval, but someone was concerned by Riana's tone of voice.

"Riana, I told you this commission would change you," Kim heard a woman say. "You have to keep a distance."

"It hasn't changed me," Riana exclaimed.

*You bet it has*, thought Kim, flicking the water off her hands. At home Riana had been an ordinary journalist. She covered human interest stories and freak events of nature, like avalanches and floods. Covering the Truth and Reconciliation Commission was different. In fact, Riana had already received hate mail and threats from locals for reporting on the commission. As Oom Piet had warned them, some people didn't like the fact that the Truth Commission was digging up the past. The notes said things like "Go home, foreign bitch," or "The communists have taken over your mind. Damn your rubbishy lies." These notes, which Kim saw by accident when she moved a pile of her mom's messy papers, were written in blood-red lettering, and they frightened her.

Kim realized that the work her mother did was harder than anything she had done before. Riana filed two or three stories a day. Riana knew that her Canadian reports were also broadcast in South Africa and that some people would hate her for

what she wrote. But she went on, letting relatives
and survivors tell, in their own words, what had happened to them. Just yesterday, she had interviewed a
white family who had been bombed in a church
two years earlier. The youngest child had been flung
from one end of the church to the other and his
body was left unrecognizable, even to his mother.

Another mother, a black journalist, had told
Riana how her fourteen-year-old son had been
arrested in the apartheid days for distributing political pamphlets. He was put in a refrigerator at the
police station for half an hour and then given an
electric shock. This story made Kim sick and the
thought of it kept her awake at night. While she was
awake she would worry about her mother.

The Truth Commission stories were so discon-
certing that a therapist had been hired to help the
journalists. Kim was aware that Riana had spoken a
couple of times with the therapist. The therapist
encouraged the journalists to talk amongst themselves about the disturbing stories rather than burden
their families. Since that time Riana often invited
colleagues home with her at the end of the day.

From the back window of the kitchen Kim
could see that a storm was building. Not just the
sloppy downpour they had had all week. Tonight the
rain was noisy and precise, accompanied by a vicious
wind. She wondered if she should go into the living

room and warn Riana's colleagues about the deteri-
orating weather.

At that moment, Riana opened the swinging
door that separated the kitchen from the living area.
Reeking of her colleagues' smoke, she shuffled into
the kitchen with the teapot in her hands. Kim hardly
recognized her mom. Riana was pale and she moved
like a sleepwalker.

"There's going to be a storm," Kim said. "Mom!"

Riana did not answer. She set the teapot down
and fired up the gas under the kettle. Kim watched
her take out a jar and spread marmite onto some
crackers. When she lifted a plate out of the cupboard, it slipped from her fingers with a crash.

Kim saw that her mom's hands were shaking.
"Riana, are you okay?" she asked.

"I can't get that woman's crying out of my
head," Riana said.

"What woman?" Kim asked.

"The mother," Riana responded. "She told me
there was a purple birthmark on her son's right knee.
It was the only way she could identify him." Riana
covered her mouth and grew silent. "I shouldn't be
telling you this."

Riana never told Kim the gruesome circumstances of the stories she worked on, but Kim sometimes found out details by overhearing the tapes that
her mom compiled for her producer.

"Riana, you need a break," Kim said. "Let's take up Uncle Piet's offer and go to the farm for a few days."

The mention of the farm got the same reaction as the word *grenade* might have. Riana jerked herself to attention.

"Correct me if I'm wrong, but didn't you promise me back home that we would visit Milky Way Farm?" Kim asked.

Riana burrowed through the cupboards. She produced a bottle of whiskey and put it on the tray with some glasses. Then, without making tea, she flicked off the gas on the stove.

"Don't leave the garden," Riana said, as she set the plate of marmite crackers on the tray. Without another word she turned and left the kitchen.

Kim wanted to shake her mother so hard that the real her would wake up and life could go on as before. Kim did not know the best way to solve her mom's problems. If Riana caught malaria in Africa, Kim swore it would be different. People died from this disease and Kim would do whatever it took to nurse her mother back to health. But this was not malaria! And the only solution was to convince her mom to stop working in South Africa and return early to Canada. Riana would never agree to that.

Suddenly there was a sharp knock on the kitchen door and Kim jerked back to reality. Her heart thumped. She was as edgy as Riana. If she didn't watch it, *she* would need a therapist too.

She pulled back the curtain to see who it was and exhaled to let the tension out as she reached for the doorknob. It was Themba.

# SIX

# CAPE OF STORMS

**K**im pulled Themba into the kitchen. He was soaked, and she handed him a clean dishtowel to dry off with. "Kim! Kim! Did you forget how to count yet?" Themba asked wiping off his face. It was wonderful to hear Themba's deep melodic voice.

She took a breath and began. "*Inye. Zimbini. Zintathu.*"

"Hey," he said, impressed.

It was only this week that he had taught her to count in Xhosa. She had forgotten four and five but didn't want him to know that.

"Kim, listen. How many Van der Merwes does it take to –"

"I'm not falling for that," she said, cutting him off. Themba had told her that her surname – Van der Merwe – was so common that it was a national joke in South Africa. Even in Canada she hated it, a name she thought to be better suited to tractors or lawn mowers than human beings.

It was just like her mother to give Kim *her* surname and not her father's. Probably her dad had an ordinary English name.

"I have good news for you," Themba said. "Themba Bandla has come up with a plan to find out more about your father."

"Sh," she warned. "Mom is in the next room." She pulled out a stool for him. "What's the plan?"

"Remember how your ma is coming this Sunday to the township to interview my neighbor, Mrs. Bansi?"

Kim nodded. Riana was very grateful that Themba had suggested the interview.

"My plan is this," continued Themba. "I'll try my best to get your ma alone and fire off a question or two about your father."

"You can try," Kim said, lowering her voice. "But from my experience, she won't tell you."

"We need to make her," Themba said. "We need to disarm her until she lets drop one little detail like his age, job, whereabouts, maybe even his name."

There was a thumping that built in her chest whenever they talked about the possibility of finding her father.

"Don't you have predictions about who he is?" he asked. "A professional athlete? A circus performer? A teacher?"

"I don't know," said Kim. She noticed that whenever Themba mentioned the search, he became animated.

"What else do we have?" he asked.

"My mom gave me a notebook that belonged to my father," said Kim. "The writing is illegible. But on the back page I noticed he wrote the word Africa spelt with a *K*. What do you make of it?"

"Maybe he's European." suggested Themba. "A German baron? A Polish count?"

Kim shrugged. "He's South African, born and raised. I know that much."

"We'll find him," said Themba. Kim appreciated Themba's offer. She wished she could do something as important for him. Suddenly, she had an idea.

"Maybe when my mom interviews your neighbor we can find out something new about your father's disappearance," she said.

There was a pause. It went on so long that Kim jumped in to fill it. "Themba?"

"I'm here," he said staring out the burglar bars.

"Maybe there will be a new detail you hadn't heard."

Themba sat up tall and stiff on the stool. His entire expression had changed. "There will not," he said with a cold voice. "I've heard Mrs. Bansi's story a million times and can't stomach to hear it once more."

The sharp edge to his voice alarmed her. Kim was sorry to have brought up his father.

Themba jumped off the stool. "I have to go." He paused to make sure she had his full attention before he said, "I've got a soccer game down at the Arena. Blokes only."

Filled with envy, Kim said nothing.

"Give a message to your Oom Piet," Themba said at the door. His anger intensified when he mentioned her uncle's name. "Tell him that his shack's roof is leaking," he said. A second later he was gone.

Her mood dropped the moment she heard the back gate crash shut. Was it *her* fault Lettie and Themba lived in her backyard and that their roof leaked? And why did Themba mention Oom Piet's name like that?

More than anything, she hated the way Themba had brought up the soccer match. Beside the back door was the calendar where she had ticked off each day since their arrival. Today was July 30th – back home it was the middle of summer. She normally played soccer every day in the summer. Her heart pulled at the memory. "Ready, over here!" she would bellow, and on cue, one of her teammates would pass the ball to her. The perfection of those passes – the thrill of moving the ball successfully from one teammate to another – was almost as intense as scoring a goal. Yet when Kim tried to scroll down the faces of

the girls on the team, she could barely recall them.
No doubt whatsoever – in the time she had been
gone they would have forgotten her.

Outside, the wind snapped the bare branches
against the glass. She shivered. The cottage was a
freezer. It was amazing how quickly it got dark. "You
keep me a prisoner in here," she had told her mom
more than once.

Kim saw the light on in Lettie's room at the end
of the garden. Nobody, not even Riana, could stop
Kim from roaming around her own garden! Kim
stuffed her feet into her rain boots and ran through
the wet shrubs to Lettie's room. Why bother to leave
a note? Let her mother put two and two together.

Lettie stood beside a hotplate. Despite the rain,
she had the top half of her wooden, two-piece door
propped open.

"Hello, Kim," she said. "Is your mom at home?"

Kim nodded and shrugged off the question.

"Come right in," said Lettie, moving a pile of
clothes off the end of her bed. Lettie wore an apron
and two sweaters over her uniform. On her head
was her navy woolen beret.

Kim sat on the bed and watched as Lettie
emptied her tea bag into the garbage and wiped out
the cup with a dishrag. Kim's stomach growled. Her
stomach said precisely how she felt – empty and
drained.

"Biscuit?" Lettie asked, pulling a canister down from a shelf.

Kim eagerly helped herself to a cookie. She leaned back against the wall and munched it. By now she knew Lettie's room by heart. There was a bed, a stool, an enamel hotplate, a cupboard, and a fold down cot that Themba used when he slept here. A worn woven rug covered most of the concrete floor. Outside the small room stood an outhouse and a tap for washing. Lettie kept saying she aimed to white-wash the place, but she never got around to it. Instead, she'd plastered magazine pictures on the walls.

Kim took a second cookie. "Themba told me that the roof is leaking," she said as she brushed the crumbs from her mouth. "I'll tell my uncle."

Lettie lifted her eyebrows to indicate a tin bucket that was catching the leak. "Don't bother your uncle," she said, as she sat down heavily on her stool. "Themba is good at school, but it is an expensive school. He has only been there for one year and he must work very hard to keep up. We are very lucky that your uncle pays the fees."

"Oom Piet pays Themba's school fees?" This was the first time she had heard this information. She remembered how angry Themba was when he spit out her uncle's name.

Lettie nodded. "Those students need two of everything. Two school blazers, two shorts, two shirts, two long pants." Lettie clicked her tongue against the side of her cheek and added. "Then there are the books."

Kim tried to concentrate on Lettie's words, but the skeleton trees clawed against the side of the tin roof, distracting her. Suddenly she had an idea. *Why didn't I think of this before?* she wondered. "You knew my mother and uncle in the old days, didn't you?" Kim asked, louder than necessary.

"Eh?" Lettie's eyes fastened on Kim's as if she saw a ghost. Then she composed herself and looked away. She said, "I grew up on the farm that belongs to their father. My ma, my sisi and her children still live there."

Kim stopped chewing and sat very still on the bed. "What year did you come to Cape Town?" She held her breath and waited. If only Lettie had come before 1983, the year Riana left for Canada, she might have known Kim's father!

"Let's see," Lettie sat in such a way that her apron stretched like an old elastic across her bare thighs. "It was early in 1984," she said. "I know the date, because I met Sandile soon after, and Themba was born at the very end of the year."

Kim's heart sank. Lettie had come to Cape Town just after Riana left for Canada. And since Riana had left the farm years earlier, there was no hope that Lettie knew her father.

Lettie flicked on her radio. After a moment she spoke. "Do you think your ma will be missing you?"

Was Lettie trying to change the subject or just get rid of her? That wouldn't be too surprising, since Kim had spent most of her evenings that week in Lettie's room.

"She needs you," continued Lettie. "She works too hard and I worry about her."

"Oh, sure," Kim said. "I'd worry too, if it wasn't so stupid."

"Stupid?" Lettie asked.

"Yeah, stupid," snapped Kim. Suddenly her breath was raspy and uneven as if she had been running a marathon. "Themba's right. This commission allows killers to get off scot-free. And the stories that the journalists have to cover are so awful that they need therapists to help them sleep at night."

Kim was surprised at how the words whipped out of her. The mention of Themba's name reminded her of her earlier blunder in the kitchen. Would Themba ever forgive her for the suggestion about his father? "I hate this Truth Commission!" she added.

Lettie took the finger-smudged butcher's calendar on which she marked her days down and fanned her face with it. "I love our country," she said. Her smooth brown skin was flushed. "I am proud to be a South African. But this wasn't always

a good country, and your ma knows this, and she
must tell these stories. Themba must get some sense.
He must stop being so troublesome. He has not
been to the bush, and will not have his initiation for
a couple of years yet. He is still a child, but he tries
to sound like a man."

Kim began to kick her sneaker toe against the
bedframe. She didn't want to be caught between
Themba and his mother. Then she remembered that
Lettie supported the commission and had decided
to attend the upcoming hearing to find out what
had happened to her husband.

Kim softened her words. "Themba told me
that if a killer appears before the commission and
confesses to a crime he will not have to go to jail,"
she said.

Lettie dunked the corner of her dishcloth into
a tub of water and wiped down the small corner
table.

"He might get amnesty," said Lettie. "That is
true."

"What's amnesty?"

Lettie lifted her eyes so they were level with
Kim's. "A pardon," she said.

"He will be free to walk away?" Kim asked.

Lettie tucked the dishcloth under her arm. "In
Xhosa the word *uxolelwano* means 'to forgive.' It is
something Sandile, my husband, believed in."

Kim was about to say something, but she stopped herself. Instead she jumped off the bed and faced Lettie squarely.

"Maybe you are right," Kim said. "Maybe Themba should go to the hearing. He is stubborn not to go. I know nothing about my father. He is a big mystery to me, and if I thought I could find out one scrap of information, I would go to ten hearings if necessary."

Lettie stared into the garden as if she didn't want to look at Kim. Somewhere in a nearby yard, one angry bark set off a dog alarm that rebounded through the entire neighborhood.

"When it comes to a father," said Lettie as Kim got ready to leave, "it is worth knowing the truth."

# SEVEN

# MOLO!

Riana pulled the car onto the dusty shoulder to let a noisy van full of people pass.

"It's not much farther," said Themba. He sat beside Kim in the backseat, but he had been directing the car since they left Cape Town.

"I hope this is a good idea," Riana said, as she steered the car back onto the road.

"Coming to the township is the best idea I've had all week," said Andries. Andries sat beside Riana in the front squinting into the noon-day sun as his tanned arm dangled out of the window. Between his fingertips he squeezed a cigarette that trailed smoke.

Could Kim be flipping out, or was Riana actually smiling across at Andries? "Andries, it wasn't your idea," said Riana kindly. "It was Themba's."

"Oh ja," Andries agreed with a shrug.

Andries had insisted on coming along, not only to help with the story, but for protection. He was one of Riana's colleagues. Kim's least favorite of her mother's colleagues. Problem number one: He had rambled nonstop for the twenty minutes since they'd left Cape Town. When he wasn't blabbing about one big happening story or another, he was chain-smoking. When he wasn't smoking, he gobbled potato chips, which he referred to as crisps, pausing every so often to chew the salt out from under his fingernails. On one occasion he passed the all-but-empty chip bag back to Kim and Themba.

From the backseat Kim studied her mother. For three days Riana had appeared almost normal. Except for the smoking. Riana, a health nut, had turned to late-night — and secret — smoking! Kim decided, for the moment, to turn a blind eye.

There were still two months remaining until they returned to Canada. Surely that was long enough to find her father. Kim hoped that Themba would find out something new on this trip.

"What if we're intruding?" muttered Riana, her eyes on the road. "Themba, you'll let us know if we're intruding."

"Yes, Mrs. van der Merwe," Themba said. To Kim it appeared as if Themba was shrinking deeper into himself. The closer they got to the township, the quieter he became. They were going to the house where Themba lived with his sister and grandfather, to the home where Lettie returned each weekend. Riana and Andries planned to inter view Lettie's neighbor, Mrs. Bansi. She had been home the night Themba's father was taken away by the police. The realization of this interview was obviously upsetting Themba.

Riana must have been thinking the same thing. She glanced at the rearview mirror. "Themba, do you remember much about the night your father disappeared?" she asked in a gentle voice.

"I was six," said Themba looking out the window. "Mrs. Bansi came afterwards to get me and my sister and took us to her house."

"I see," said Riana. Her eyes flicked back to the road.

Kim began to dread this trip. She knew that Lettie had not been home at the time of the abduction because she had been working at Oom Piet's cottage. Kim wondered whether, if Lettie had been there, things might have worked out differently.

The car turned onto a bumpy road. "Look at this mess," Riana said as she helped herself to the broken remains at the bottom of Andries' chip bag. On the outskirts of the township was a wide-open field where people had used bits of cardboard, plastic, metal odds and ends, whatever they could find, to make a patchwork of shelters.

The road into the township didn't look any better. Kim had never been inside a township: she was shocked to see shacks and small cement houses built almost on top of each other. Newspapers and rusted cans rolled down the street or into a ditch filled with stagnant water. Nearby, three boys whirled an old car tire between them, chasing it with a stick. Riana kept slowing down so as not to cover the boys with dust.

Riana wiped broken chips from the front of her sweater. "I never thought I'd set foot in a location," she said with a nervous laugh.

"Township," Andries corrected her, as he took a deep drag on his cigarette. "Riana, we call them townships now." Kim couldn't stand this guy. When he smoked his eyes narrowed into slits.

Kim flinched as the smoke drifted back. She tried to catch Themba's eye, but he was still staring out the window. She followed his gaze and looked at his Afrika, the place where he'd grown up and still lived.

"Is this a school?" Riana asked as they passed a long low building. There were children, some no taller than Kim's waist, playing everywhere in the street. Riana slowed to a crawl to avoid hitting anyone.

"It was my primary school," said Themba.

Kim studied the red brick building. There was rusted chain-link fencing around the school and almost all of the square windows were shattered. She couldn't imagine going to a school like this. She knew that when Riana was a student, she was with white children only, in a school with a library, swimming pool, and good teachers. Mixed race and Indian kids went to separate, second-rate schools. Black kids, like Themba, went to the worst schools, where there were few books and pencils and no notebooks or desks. She herself had gone to a sparkling new school in north Calgary and had never thought much about it. Surrounded by the ugly cement houses and poor children pushing up close to the car, Kim felt more and more uncomfortable by the minute.

"*Molo*," said Themba. "Welcome to Langa! It's the house at the end of the street."

Riana stopped in front of a small cement dwelling with a tin roof. "Don't leave the street," she told Kim. "I want to be able to see you from this house at all times."

"Okay," said Kim and Themba as they got out of the car. Riana and Andries opened their notebooks and leaned in together. They were going over what they were going to ask Mrs. Bansi about the night Sandile was taken.

Kim and Themba had not gone two steps before a swarm of boys charged up to them. She felt the full force of their eyes on her. Her heart began to pound.

Themba stood close to her. "Themba Bandla is here," he shouted. "Where's the ball? Let's play."

Soccer! It was exactly what Kim needed. Teams

were formed quickly. Yet when Kim tried to join in, the township boys stared her down.

Themba put himself between Kim and the youths. "Let her play," he ordered. Makeshift goal-posts were two large tin garbage cans at one end, old tires at the other. It was the middle of the day and the sun was very hot.

The ball was thrown in and the boys went after it. Kim wanted to immerse herself in the game and forget her mounting fear. She had heard stories of township gangs that killed Whites. As long as she was with Themba, she was safe – wasn't she?

She kept her speed down and tried to get the feel of the dusty ground. "Mine," boasted one boy as he sprinted after the ball. "Zola, over here," bellowed his teammate. They were all speaking English – maybe to include her.

The ball was kicked in her direction. Kim kept her eyes on it and her mind on scoring. Guarding the ball between her feet, she weaved through three boys and ran hard. She belted the ball with her foot. *Whack!* She adored the smack of the ball on the side of her shoe. Usually it meant success. Today was no exception. She scored! There were cheers, and Themba's voice was the loudest.

A car passed and interrupted the game for a moment. Kim stood back from the others and panted.

"Is this Kim?" a tall girl in an orange dress suddenly appeared behind Themba. She was slim, long-limbed, and pretty. Her lips were the color of plums.

Themba nodded. "Kim," he said, "this is my sister, Sophie."

"Mmm, hello," Sophie murmured shyly. Little kids crowded in beside her.

"Kim is from Canada," Themba told everyone.

*Thank you for not telling them my surname*, Kim thought. Tension melted from her body as she re-tied her hair back from her face. To these African kids she was the Canadian girl with the strange accent who played soccer. None of them knew that her relatives were Afrikaners, the very people who had set up the system that for many years controlled their lives. She hoped she could trust Themba to keep her secret.

The ball bounced down the street and every-one ran after it. Kim ran the hardest and the fastest. Her lungs were sore and the midday sun was hot.

"Give," mumbled a tall boy who jerked in front of her. He snuck the ball away and ran with it. When Kim swivelled to follow him, her ankle gave way. She tripped and stumbled chin-first onto the sandy ground. Her elbow landed in mud – or was it dog dirt? Clumsy clout!

Themba pushed through the crowd and helped Kim to her feet.

"I'm okay," she said, standing up to show everyone that her ankle was fine. The truth was, her ankle was throbbing, and she had to grab onto Themba's arm for support.

"Take a moment. Can you stand on it?" Themba asked.

"It's okay," Kim insisted, even though she winced with pain.

"Kim, come on," he said. "Let's take a break. Go inside. Sophie will help you. I'll go next door and get you some ice. It will give me a chance to talk to your ma."

Every bone in Kim's body wanted to continue playing soccer, but unless she hobbled around using Sophie as a crutch, it was impossible. Sophie stepped forward to help. She had an easy, loose walk and probably would have been great at soccer if only she had been asked to play.

"Themba, tell my mom where I am," Kim yelled across the small yard. Behind her she heard Themba's musical voice in the street, calling, "Bye Johnny. Bye Thami. Bye Zola."

"Don't mention my ankle," she added with a shout.

The front door of Themba's home had been left open. The house was small and perfectly square. The main room was overcrowded with furniture. Along one side was a low book case, and there were some photos on the wall. Sophie led her to the sofa.

"Thanks," said Kim, wincing.

An African man entered the room carrying a couple of Cokes. He had short gray tufts of hair and bright eyes. He was dressed formally, like a minister or schoolteacher. "Welcome," he said staring at Kim. Sophie spoke to him in the clicking language before she waved good-bye to Kim and left. "Sophie has gone down the street to the shops," he said. "You must be Kim. I'm Themba's grandfather. Grandpa Khan-yi-sa."

"Khan-yi-sa," repeated Kim.

"With African names you pronounce all the letters," he said handing her a Coke. He looked down at her sneakers admiring them. "Heavens. I've never seen *tackies* like that before. And now the township dust has soiled them."

"That's okay," Kim said.

She took a drink of Coke and looked around her. Before they moved to the bungalow, she and Riana had lived in a cramped apartment, but there were only two of them. Themba's house was even smaller, and he lived with Sophie, his grandfather, and Lettie on weekends.

Kim glanced up at a large framed poster on the wall. "That's the Freedom Charter," explained Themba's grandfather. "The charter was created in

1955 and it declares that South Africa belongs to all who live in it."

"Black *and* white?" Kim asked. She remembered the fear she experienced earlier on the township street.

He returned her gaze. "Yes," he said.

She sipped her Coke.

Grandpa Khanyisa cleared his throat and spoke, "Themba was eight when he memorized all those words. Themba Bandla was an eager student back then. He even tried to write a composition about the Freedom Charter in Standard One. The composition ended with the cry for freedom: *Amandla!* My daughter, Lettie, and I ordered that he burn the composition."

"Why?" she asked.

But it wasn't Grandpa Khanyisa who answered. Themba spoke loudly as he entered the room. "*Amandla* means 'power,'" he said. "They were scared of the white inspector who supervised our township school." Themba was holding a small bucket of ice and he had a deep frown on his face. "After what happened to Pa, they were scared."

Grandpa Khanyisa was startled by Themba's voice. "Why don't you announce yourself instead of listening at the door," he said sharply.

Themba's eyes narrowed. "Kim needs to hear this," he said. "Many of our parents and grandparents were scared of the former government and the police. But not my father."

Kim watched Themba's grandfather take a matchstick from his mouth in disgust. Grandpa Khanyisa spoke first: "We wanted change, but disapproved of some of the young people's tactics." He turned to Kim and clicked his tongue on the side of his cheek. "We saw little girls scar their hands and faces for good, trying to set fire to buses. We saw their brothers blinded by stones that were thrown in the wrong direction. In my day, young people were taught to pay attention to their elders."

A phone rang in another room and Themba's grandfather got slowly to his feet. Kim was relieved when he left the room and the tension would end. She watched Themba carefully line up some ice cubes in the middle of a cloth. "What's up next door?" she asked.

"They have finished the interview," said Themba. He sat beside her on the sofa and stretched out his long legs.

"And my mom? Did you get anything out of her?"

"I found out something," he said as he held the cloth up to her ankle. "How's that?"

"Better," she answered. His eyes caught hers. It was almost as if the anger toward his grandfather had released the tension inside him and calmed him.

"After the interview was over Andries was bugging your mom for a date. He said to her: 'It's been a long time since you've been with that would-be writer.'" Themba held the ice in place. "I bet that's your father."

Kim remembered that her mother had told her this detail when she gave her the notebook. "My mom told me he wanted to be a writer."

"We could check libraries and book stores but we need a first and a last name."

"I'll try," Kim said. "Thanks."

Themba continued to press the cloth against her ankle. Kim noticed how pale her skin was against his black hand. There was a pause.

"Thanks for not telling those kids my surname," she said. She kept her eyes fixed on her ankle instead of looking at him.

"You're safe with me," Themba responded.

There was more silence. Kim looked around the room. Her eyes rested on a framed photo on the table beside the sofa.

"Is that your father?" Kim asked. The man in the photo had dark skin and Themba's teasing eyes.

With his free hand Themba lifted the photo and showed it to Kim. "Yes," said Themba. "He was a freedom fighter. He and many others fought for the freedom we have today."

Kim didn't know what to say. Her ankle throbbed as Themba moved the ice around to the top of her foot. She picked up her Coke.

"The curious thing is, I knew something was going to happen that night," Themba said. He looked over his shoulder to make sure his grandfather was still in the other room. "I woke up shivering, even though it was a hot night. When I heard the sound of the gravel under the police van, I pulled Sophie under the bed with me. It was the middle of the night – another kind of dark – Sophie was four and I was six. Ma was not there – nor was my grandfather – so I had to take care of my sister."

Kim put down her Coke bottle. She was trying to concentrate on Themba's words. They came out slow and gentle as if he was talking about something that had happened to someone else.

"In two seconds they had kicked down the front door, shattered a window, and marched like beasts out the back door. Under the bed I held Sophie tightly so she would not cry. She peed all over me."

He was sitting very close to Kim and continued to hold the ice in place on her ankle. His fingers trembled. "After a few minutes I crawled up to the window and pressed my eye against the glass," he said. "They found my father hiding in the back shed. I could see in the light from the headlights that Pa's

ear was bleeding. His eye was hurt – swollen shut –
like the eye that wouldn't open on Sophie's doll. He
was dressed in his underwear and there was something like ma's old *lappie* stuffed in his mouth." He
paused, swallowed, and then added. "They threw
him in the back of the van like a dog."

Kim chewed on a hangnail. Her cheeks were
hot. She wanted to take the ice out of Themba's
hands and rub it over her face.

"That was the last I ever saw of him," Themba
added.

Kim turned so sharply that she almost upset
her Coke. She forced herself to stay seated. This had
happened with Lettie too. Sometimes Lettie's troubles were so huge and distressing that Kim felt like
fleeing from her presence like a thief.

She wanted to say something to Themba, but
no words came. She wanted to put her hand out and
touch him, but her limbs were frozen. Instead, she
stared out the window where Themba had watched
his father disappear. Riana and Andries had returned
to the car. Andries was smoking, leaning up against
the passenger door. Kim saw her mother rake her
fingers through her hair as if to soothe a building
headache.

Kim had never felt this close to Themba. She
remembered his earlier words, *You're safe with me* and
how his voice had reassured her. Yet she did not have

a single word of comfort for him. Instead she said something inane and distant in a voice that was not unlike her own mother's. "I'm sorry." She got to her feet and left.

# EIGHT

# THE FIGHT

"**W**hat are you going to do today while I'm in school?" Kim asked her mother as she adjusted the tie on her school uniform.

Riana slumped into her chair and muttered, "Huh?"

*Lord, she's really losing it now*, Kim thought. Her mother was not even out of the old checked shorts and white T-shirt that she slept in. In fact, she had been in the same clothes for a couple of days in a row. Her hair, unbrushed and unwashed, was a complete mess. The house was freezing. The kitchen tiles were ice-cold. Kim wondered if Riana was even okay to be left on her own. She guessed that her mother would probably sit there until Lettie came to make her a cup of the orange-red rooibos tea that Riana loved so much.

"Mom, you need to pull yourself together," Kim said, grabbing her school blazer from the back of the chair and pulling it on. "Where are your shoes? Have you answered Oom Piet's phone messages?"

Riana glanced dully across at her.

It was no use. Riana would have a couple of good days where she would throw herself into her work with ferocious energy, and all would appear sane. Then, without warning, she would explode into hysterics or crash into inactive silence.

Now there were the nightmares to contend with. Kim never remembered Riana having sleeping problems before and it frightened her. "Last night you had a nightmare supreme," Kim told her.

"I did?"

"You cried out," Kim said. "Then you talked – shouted – in your sleep. It was your second nightmare this week. Don't you remember?"

Riana shook her head, unable to call it up. In addition to the interview with Themba's neighbor, she was working on a particularly difficult story about a woman, a member of a previously banned organization, whose teenage daughter had lost four fingers and an eye when a parcel had exploded in her hands. The package had been meant for the woman, not the girl, a detail that deeply upset not only the mother of the injured girl, but Riana as well.

Riana drew her legs beneath her to keep her feet off the cold kitchen floor. "Kim," she said, "we need to talk about something."

Kim sat down across from her. "No more smoking, Mom. That's what we need to talk about."

Last night Kim had gotten up in the middle of the night because she thought she smelled something burning. She found her mom in the chair near the fireplace smoking cigarettes with a full ashtray in her lap.

Riana blinked twice and then looked at Kim, frightened. "Okay. Fine. But . . ." she began, then stopped.

"What?" Kim searched her mother's face trying to predict what was coming. Riana's unwashed hair appeared more dark than blonde, and there were circles under her eyes.

"They want me to stay for a bit longer."

Kim practically fell off her chair. "What?"

"They want me for three more mon —"

"Who's they – Andries?"

"Not *Andries*. My producer."

"Are you out of your skull?" Kim fired back. "You are already waking up nights scared to death. We'll be lucky if you survive the remaining five weeks, never mind three more months!"

Riana's cell phone rang and she jammed the phone to her ear. "Ja, Ja, I will, ja, I will try," she said into her cell.

Kim jumped to her feet, remembered her ankle was still sore, and grabbed the kitchen table for support. She was amazed to see her mother on the phone conducting business. As if everything was fine! Was it her imagination or had Riana's accent become stronger in the six weeks since they had been here? It didn't take a genius to figure it out: first it would be three months, and then six months, then who knows how long? Kim might never see Canada again.

Riana flipped her cell closed and turned to face her daughter.

"Kim, you're doing fine. I mean, I'm so proud of how you're making out in your new school."

"I hate that school." Kim cried.

"What about your new friends?"

"What friends?"

"Marjorie. Themba."

"Marjorie is *not* a friend," Kim said. "And Themba is . . . different."

Kim's face flushed as she spoke Themba's name. Riana glanced quickly into the garden.

"He's not here," Kim told her. "He had soccer last night and stayed in the township."

Riana turned back to her daughter. "Kim, journalists are here from all over the world. It is an honor to report on this."

"Something's the matter with you," Kim said gripping the edge of the table. "In Canada you weren't like this: smoking, nightmares, forgetting to get dressed in the mornings. Everything makes you sad. You, like, *seesaw* from one emotion to another."

"My therapist said it was no good running from the commission. She says I have to stay and face it."

"Five weeks, Mom. That's enough time left for you to face whatever you need to face."

"Kim, please."

"No!" shouted Kim. "I won't stay here one day longer than we agreed on!"

Before Riana could respond, a car honked. What perfect luck: it was Marjorie's mother. Today – an exception – Kim took three, eager, let-me-out-of-here strides toward the car, ignoring the pain in her ankle. Riana tried to catch her arm, but missed. Kim slammed the door and, wincing slightly, made her way down the gravel driveway to the street.

Kim's anger at her mother reminded her of the dream that had shaken her awake the night before. In the dream, she was running after a man whose face she could not see, and he was getting away from her. Kim kept trying to reach out to him, but her arms were heavy as if weighted down, and her legs were deep in quicksand. She woke to darkness, her heart pounding, a tangle of sheets around her sweaty body.

Kim got into the back of Marjorie's car, trying to shake off the memory of the dream. It didn't take a genius to figure out who the running man was. In Canada she had hardly ever thought about her father, let alone dreamt of him. Once, a girl back home who couldn't stop talking about her own father and an amazing ski trip they had gone on together, had asked Kim about her dad. Kim had been cool and noncommittal. "He left before I was born," she had said.

The girl had been shocked.

"We were the ones who left, actually," Kim quickly told her. "My mother left him before I was born." This explanation hadn't made any difference to the girl, but the declaration that they had deserted *him* made Kim feel better.

"After school, I might have some girls over for tea," said Marjorie, interrupting her thoughts. "Could you come?"

What did Marjorie, with her yellow hair and very proper accent, think of her? "I can't," Kim said, turning away from Marjorie's crystal blue eyes. "I'm playing soccer with Themba."

Marjorie's mouth fell open. It was the first time Kim noticed Marjorie was wearing lipstick. They drove the rest of the way to the school in silence. But when they reached the school grounds and climbed out of the car, Marjorie put one hand on her waist and said, "Watch out. Don't ever be alone with him. Our Blacks aren't the same as yours."

A new wave of anger washed over Kim. But before she could say a word to defend Themba, Marjorie strolled away from her, toward her tight clique of girlfriends. Resisting the urge to baby her ankle, Kim found herself running hard and fast toward the field at the side of the school. A pleasant feeling of exertion spread through her. Sometimes, like right now, all she wanted to do was get away from everything: her mother, the commission, Marjorie. On the edge of the field, in front of a group of boys who were kicking a soccer ball, was Themba.

"Anything the matter?" he asked seeing her face.

Kim caught her breath and said, "My mom's crazy. She wants to stay here a few more months and I want to leave – today!"

"Leave today? What about your pa?"

At that moment, Kim found the soccer ball in her path. She kicked it with a satisfying *whack*. Her ankle was back in working order. "I just want to go home," she yelled. "I don't care if he is dead or alive!"

Themba dug his hands into his hips. "Be careful what you say. If it were *my* father, I would want to know everything. Every single detail."

"Then why tell your mom you won't go to the hearing," she shouted, angry all over again. "Your mom wants you to go, but you keep saying no!"

His eyes flashed. "Keep quiet," he snapped. "Keep quiet about things . . . you . . . know . . . nothing . . . about!" He jerked past her to join the soccer game.

His words – spat out like that – felt like a punch in the stomach. For a moment Kim was immobilized. *Get out of here*, she told herself. *Get away, before you kill someone.* She was about to turn and run when suddenly, James, the short boy with the gigantic ears, was right up beside her. "*Kaffir-lover*," he hissed, his cheeks rosy from running.

"What did you say?" Kim shouted. She saw Themba in the far corner of the field.

Elephant Ears spoke louder, "I said, sissie girl, go home."

Kim lunged forward. Before she could think, her fist lifted and she clobbered James down to the ground.

James put up one knee, shifted his weight onto it and stood. His face red and furious, he came at Kim.

Kim was ready for him. Her emotions were churning inside her and she felt very strong. She crashed her fists one, two, three solid punches to his face, chin and chest. James tumbled down.

Kids gathered around. James rose to his feet again, but did not come back at her. Clearly shocked, he took a step away, checking out his nose and chin.

Kim moved off, panting. She hoped Themba was watching.

The principal, walking at quite a clip, pushed through the circle of boys. She squared her shoulders and stood in front of Kim. "What is your name?" she asked loudly.

"Kim van der Merwe."

"How old are you?"

"Twelve," Kim gulped, "I mean thirteen." She was mixed up as she tried to slow down her breath.

The principal was furious. "I cannot stress enough how inappropriate this behavior is," she said. Then she escorted Kim off the field and into the school. A group of kids followed behind them. They were eager to see what trouble she would get into. The principal shooed them off irritably. "It's over," she said.

A few minutes later, from the window of the principal's office, Kim watched her mother arrive at the entrance. When the caretaker opened the gates, Riana stumbled forward. Kim noticed that her mom had changed her pants and put on shoes, but was still in the same white T-shirt that she'd slept in. She had woven a scarf around her unwashed hair. "You stay right here," the principal said, as she went to meet Riana.

Kim rubbed her hand across her mouth and waited for what felt like a long time. She knew she was too old to be fighting, but clobbering James made her feel reckless and powerful. She really hoped that Themba had seen how angry she was. She also hoped this fight would convince her mother that they could not remain three extra months in South Africa.

Riana was quiet and pale when the principal finally led her into the office. She appeared as if *she* were the one to have had the breath knocked out of her. The principal pursed her lips and spoke. "Your mother tells me that you are not very happy in our school. You need to talk over your problems and not bring them into the schoolyard."

"Yes, Miss," Kim said.

"I'm afraid that I must suspend you for a week." The principal looked grimly from Kim to her mother. "As you well know, in this country we are trying to solve our problems with negotiations, not violence. If anything like this happens again I will be forced to expel your daughter."

Silently, Kim followed her mother out the door and past the deserted tennis courts and manicured lawn. In a moment they were sitting in the car outside the schoolyard, the tall iron gates locked behind them. Kim took three or four swallows from Riana's water bottle. She couldn't believe how good it felt to be off her sore ankle.

"James is a racist pig," Kim said by way of an excuse.

Riana did not respond. She didn't shout or question. Kim was scared. It was as if her mother was having trouble understanding what had happened.

Riana's cell rang and she winced. She put the phone to her ear and listened. Her hand shook as she jabbed a loose strand of greasy, dark blonde hair under her scarf.

"Lukas, I'll try," whispered Riana and then flipped her cell closed and rested the smooth silver surface on her cheek, trying to cool it.

"What's wrong?" asked Kim.

Riana shook her head from side to side as if trying to rouse herself. "They want another sound bite from the parcel bomb story."

Kim remembered the horrible story about the mother whose teenage daughter had been so badly injured. Riana would now have to relive the interview with the distraught woman and find a quote or two that would sum up her pain and hit home to a Canadian audience.

Kim felt guilty about being suspended. Riana didn't deserve to work all day on gruesome stories and then have a kid like her to contend with!

"I'm sorry, Mom," said Kim, "I really am. Let's go home, send off the story, and then go to the beach."

"I can't! I can't," said Riana, pounding the steering wheel. "I can't – just – go – to – the – beach."

Kim was even more frightened now. Her mother was unraveling like a ball of yarn that had bounced off a table. "Mom," Kim asked gently, "are you okay to drive?"

Riana did not respond. Then, she began to cry. She made no noise, and Kim would not have noticed, except every once in a while she flipped her finger under her large glasses.

"Are you crying?" Kim asked.

"No."

It was unbelievable. Her mother, despite all her outbursts, had never once cried in front of Kim. "You are too crying."

"I am *not*."

Kim placed her hand on top of her mother's. Suddenly, an idea struck her. It was a risk, sure, but there was a soft feeling between her and her mom, a feeling that usually wasn't there. She decided to take a chance. "Maybe you'd feel better," she whispered, "if you just told me his name."

Her mother blinked twice. "Who?"

"My father," said Kim.

"Hendrik Fortune," Riana said quietly.

"That's his name?"

"Yes," said Riana.

Kim kept her hand on top of her mother's and silently repeated the name over and over so as not to forget it.

Riana swallowed twice then spoke. "I've made a decision. I will not stay on. Let's just finish up what we agreed to in the first place and leave."

"Okay," said Kim. She wondered if the principal had convinced her mother that Kim was better off in Canada.

Riana pulled her hand away and turned the car key. "I should have told you his name long ago, but I couldn't."

Kim had a million questions to ask but she needed to formulate them carefully. Coming from Riana this was a lot of information for one day. They drove in silence. They were both exhausted and the quiet was calming.

When they pulled into the driveway, Oom Piet's Land Rover was parked there. Piet was standing next to it, smoking a cigarette. Bliksem was sprawled on the driveway. The dog leaped to his feet when he saw Riana's car.

"Check how tired you are, man!" Piet said rushing up to Riana's side of the car. "Lettie tells me. You work day and night like a machine. You live off chocolate and coffee. You're getting stretched thinner and thinner until what, Riana, you snap?"

Riana stared in silence, then blew her nose.

"Listen. I had to come into town for business. Enough is enough, Riana. You have to now come home." Fired up, he glanced at Kim to include her. "It works like this, see. Red-pink-crimson sunsets that work magic on the *koppies*, the little Karoo hills, until they're etched in purple against the darkening sky. Imagine that now, Kim. And you can meet your cousins, Marjike and Japie, and old Grandpa."

Her uncle leaned into the car in anticipation. Kim couldn't help but be excited, too. She had heard about this farm since she was little and she really wanted to go.

"Mom," she pleaded. "Are you listening to Oom Piet?"

Her uncle gripped the car door as he spoke. "Riana, remember the warm, clear Karoo air? The deep blue of the heavens? The golden ball of sun in the sky?"

"Mom, I don't have school next week," Kim reminded her.

Piet waved his hand to make sure Riana was paying attention. "What about the Karoo nights, hey, Riana? And the Southern Cross in all its glory. Have you forgotten? No city lights to mar its splendor."

"Okay," said Riana with a weak smile. "I'll take next week off. We'll come."

# ROBBEN ISLAND

"**W**hy won't you tell me what this is all about?" Kim yelled as a shower of spray flew up from the stern of the ferry.

"Soon," Themba shouted above the wind.

Kim held fast to the railing as the boat slammed against the water. It was Saturday, the day before Riana and she were scheduled to leave for the farm. Themba had banged on their kitchen window and announced that he had a surprise. He had arranged for Ntombi to take them to the Cape Town harbor. He would tell Kim nothing else, but he asked her to bring her father's notebook along.

Outside on the deck, the wind was fierce. Themba moved closer to her ear. "I didn't want Ntombi to know what we're up to," he said.

Themba looked back at the dock where twenty minutes ago he and Kim had left his aunt. He had suggested that Ntombi wait for them in the dock-side café where they had bought the tickets for the trip to Robben Island. Her hair had recently been highlighted with red and braided with beads, and

Themba reminded her that she didn't want it ruined in the wind. "Go on," Ntombi had said, opening her magazine. "I don't want to see the prison. The ferry returns at three. I'll meet you back here then. Bye-bye."

Kim on the other hand, was curious. Robben Island was the site of the prison that once imprisoned President Mandela.

She watched as Cape Town – sheltered beneath that odd, flat-topped mountain – got farther and farther away and then evaporated into the fog. She felt slightly queasy from nerves, excitement, or the motion of the boat. Thankfully, Themba didn't appear to notice how green she must have looked. She didn't want anything to spoil this excursion. She was ashamed of how she had shouted at him on the school field last week, on the day of her fight with Elephant Ears. Two nights after the fight, Kim had broken down and called Themba. She was sorry about how the argument had gone. What right did she have to judge him? It was his business, not hers, if he went to the hearing about his father's death, and she told him so. Then she went on to tell him the news about her own father's name. Themba was thrilled to finally have a real clue, and he appeared to have forgotten the argument. "What's important now is finding Hendrik Fortune," he had told her.

"I have a lead about your father," he said as he

looked out to the sea. "As soon as you gave me his name I started looking at phone books. I found what I was looking for at the Cape Town library."

Kim's heart raced. She rubbed her stomach with one hand, her chest with the other. She needed to be strong and not get sick.

"A man called Hendrik Fortune lives on Robben Island," Themba added.

Kim started, but then recovered. "Are you sure?"

Themba nodded. He narrowed his eyes in the wind and did not speak for awhile. Kim wondered what was going on in his mind. Themba was a mystery to her. Why was he pushing her so hard to find her father? She suspected that this search had something to do with his feelings about his own father. Silently she watched the sea until the boat docked alongside the jetty.

They climbed off the boat. "Look at this," Themba exclaimed, squatting to pick something off the path. A child behind them bent down to see. "A *shon-go-lo-lo*," said Themba. The millipede was the width of a fat finger, with countless legs. "It's good luck," said Themba. "Maybe we'll find your father today."

"*Sies*," said the child crinkling her nose in disgust.

Even though the creature was good luck, Kim could not bring herself to touch it. Themba set it down on a lime-green aloe plant. Then he straight-ened up and peeled off his jersey. "Listen," he said as they stood in line to get on the bus. Together, they listened to the deep, melancholy sound of the harbor foghorn – a sound Kim had never heard in landlocked Alberta.

Kim followed Themba into the bus that would take them to the old prison that was now a museum. The bus driver, a balding, round, black man, ex-plained that this small island had served as a prison for four hundred years. "Criminals, political prison-ers, and lepers were exiled here," he told them.

The bus rattled and lurched along the dirt road. There were no cars, no hotels or cafés, and no shops. The landscape was flat and dusty with the occasional rock or clump of bushes that looked like upright pineapples. The island looked almost as desolate as the moon.

The bus eventually rumbled to a stop in front of the prison, but Kim remained in her seat. Her heart raced. Was she really ready to know about her father? Emotions, all of them fighting with each other, rushed at her, making it hard to breathe.

"What's the matter?" Themba asked.

She folded her arms stubbornly across her chest and remained silent. How could she explain what she was feeling?

"Come on," Themba said gently. He raised himself out of his seat. "Maybe we can find someone in the museum who knows something."

Kim followed Themba and the other visitors through the entrance into a wide-open space with a few prickly trees off to one side. The prison walls were made of huge black rocks cemented together in an irregular pattern. Kim was shocked to see how small the windows were. Set back into the rock, they were secured with thick bars. On top of one wall was a coil of vicious-looking barbed wire. The sun was burning through the fog and it was getting hot.

A thick vine had twisted itself into knots around an old clothesline. Beside it stood the guide – a thin man in a faded suit without a tie. He introduced himself as Amos, a former inmate. As he waited for everyone to form a circle around him, Themba dug his elbow into Kim's side and whispered: "When we get a chance, show him the notebook and ask him about Hendrik Fortune."

Kim peeked quickly into her knapsack to make sure her father's notebook was still there. Then she tried to listen to what the guide was saying.

"We were fed maize, cattle feed we called it, and not much else," Amos said, as the group pushed closer to him. "We slept on straw mats. We woke up early and worked for hours in the quarry, smashing rocks. It was backbreaking work, especially in the summer. Our eyes were damaged from the rock dust and the glare of the sun."

"Did anyone ever escape?" asked Themba.

The guide chuckled. "No, man. A guard tower overlooked the prison. And the mainland was too far off. Then there were the sharks. Swimming was out of the question. We talked about it though."

Amos led the group into the prison. They looked at a chart that described the meager food rations the prisoners received. Then they walked along a corridor with cells on both sides. Themba tried to get close enough to Amos to talk to him, but was cut off by the tourists.

"Here is the cell that you have all been waiting so patiently to see," Amos said, "the cell of our most famous prisoner, Madiba, also known as Nelson Mandela." He paused. When everyone was paying attention, he continued: "In 1964 Nelson Mandela was captured, imprisoned and sentenced to life imprisonment. Sabotage and plotting to overthrow the government were the charges against him. He served over twenty-seven years in jail, many of them in this modest cell. He was not allowed to have a bed until after 1978."

Kim and Themba pushed to the front. The cell was tiny. Inside there was a mat on the ground with a low stool beside it, on which sat a tin plate and cup. Resting in one corner was a gray blanket and in another, a tin bucket with a lid that served as the toilet. Kim looked at the cramped cell and thought of the man who had waited so long to be president. Now here was something to be angry about! The former government had locked him up for twenty-seven years and yet, President Mandela asked people to forgive.

"How did you end up in this prison?" asked an American tourist from the back row. "Blame my wife for my nosiness," he added. His wife, who was holding a large videocamera, blushed.

"It is my job to answer questions," Amos said. "I was a student leader and was arrested for organizing protests against the government."

"How long were you here?" Themba asked. "If you don't mind my asking."

"No, son." Amos answered. "Seven years."

"Seven years?" repeated Themba. "And are you able to show kindness toward the people who have wronged you?"

Amos smiled without answering the question and escorted the group out of the building and into a cement courtyard surrounded by high walls. The tour of the prison was over and the group moved in the direction of the bus. Themba used this moment to approach Amos. "Excuse me, we are looking for someone. Can you help us?"

It was very bright in the courtyard and Kim's eyes took a moment to adjust. As if in a trance, she dug out the notebook and handed it to Amos.

"This belonged to a man by the name of Hendrik Fortune," said Themba. "He is supposed to live on the island."

The guide turned the notebook over in his hands. Kim was relieved that Themba was doing the talking because suddenly she could not trust her voice. She looked down at her shoes and pretended disinterest.

"I know a man named Hendrik Fortune," said Amos. "We call him 'Cape Town Harry.' He's been a caretaker here for decades. You will find him near the penguins in the small bay near the boat jetty. Why do you ask?"

Before Kim could answer, Themba jumped in. "It belonged to the pa she has never met. The pa who abandoned her before she was born."

"Themba," Kim warned. She did not want him telling this stranger her whole stupid life story.

"Be careful," said Amos to Themba as he handed the notebook back to Kim. "If I learned anything in this prison it was tolerance, my son. Tolerance for other people's cultures, languages — and pain."

Themba stepped forward. "Her father, whoever he is, spells Africa with a *K* not a *C*."

Amos thought about this for a moment. "If I were writing about things related to the Bantu, our people and their lives, I might do so. I might write: 'Afrika holds a lot of sweet memories for me.' But remember, other people spell Africa with a *K*. The Afrikaner for one."

Themba nodded. "Thank you," he said. "The bus is waiting for us."

"Go well," said Amos.

On the bus Kim sat silently with the notebook on her lap. She was no longer angry at Themba for telling the guide her story. Now it was the reality of perhaps meeting her father that consumed her. Could this really be him? Her chest contracted at the thought of it. She had no idea what to say or how to act toward him. When the engine ground to a halt in front of the dock, Kim sank into her chair, frozen.

"Kim," Themba said. "We have time to go down to the bay." She sat silently and did not move. "Don't you want to see the penguins, if nothing else?"

"Okay."

Themba led her down the path toward the sea. The first thing she saw as she climbed over a dune were dozens and dozens of glossy-skinned penguins. They stood in small groups and looked at Kim regally, making no attempt to run away as she and Themba approached.

Nearby was a man in overalls and a red cap with his back to them. His faded shirt had the sleeves rolled up. He had a shovel and was cleaning up after the penguins. Themba approached him.

"*Ek soek* Hendrik Fortune," Themba said.

The man turned toward them, threw back his head, and laughed. "Fortune – dat's me. Holds lots of records for fis' caught."

This man was Hendrik Fortune! Kim looked closer at him. His skin was dark copper brown and toughened by the outdoors. His eyes were as black as night. This man could not possibly be her father. "This is a wild goose chase," she whispered to Themba.

"Wait. Give me the notebook," insisted Themba.

Themba was totally out to lunch. But Kim did as she was told and handed him the notebook. "I'm out of here!" she muttered, retreating. In fact she moved so quickly that she startled a penguin. The bird hopped off a rock and waddled on his wide feet toward the sea.

The noise of the waves filled her head so she couldn't think. The rocks were slick with the spit from the sea and she almost slipped, stepping from one boulder to the next. She suddenly felt dizzy and had to stop. She squatted, balancing herself with one hand on a rock. Out of the corner of her eye she could see that Themba was still wasting his time talking to the old man.

Sitting back on her heels, Kim picked up two shells – one smooth white mussel shell and a second pretty periwinkle. The feeling of the shells in her palm jerked at her memory. When she was young, her mother had used the dark recesses of a shell to explain the internal female body and where babies grew. What fascinated Kim the most was not the birth process but the fact that afterwards babies were kept together in a large room in the hospital. Whenever her mom struggled to bring the comb through Kim's thick curls, so different from her smooth blonde hair, Kim fired off the same question. How could Riana be so sure that she had brought home the correct baby from the hospital?

A penguin brayed like a donkey and Kim started. Then she got to her feet and waved at Themba. "Hurry up," she shouted. "I don't want to be left behind."

Ten minutes later they stood on the deck as the boat started back to Cape Town. Living up to its Cape-of-Storms reputation, the sea was much rougher than when they crossed earlier.

"Why did you run off?" Themba shouted above the wind. "His name was Fortune. He might have been your grandfather."

"Sure thing," she said stuffing the notebook into her knapsack. She spun around to look Themba right in the eye. Her cheeks were on fire. The pitching of the boat was making her stomach turn. "That man is –" she paused, furious, searching for the word.

Themba found it for her. "Colored," he said. "Is that what this is about? You are ashamed of that colored man!"

"I am not!" Kim cried.

Themba paced back and forth. "Kim! Kim! Surprise! What if your pa is of mixed race?"

"Sit down and shut up," she yelled. She was sick – couldn't he see how sick she was? If he didn't shut up she was going to puke on his foot.

"What has your mom been hiding all these years?" he yelled back. "Ask yourself that! What is the big shameful secret that she won't tell you?"

Where were the washrooms? In the lower deck of the stupid boat, no doubt.

She barely made it to the railing. The insides of her stomach spewed out of her mouth and ran pink and ugly down the stern of the boat. She gagged, coughed again, and hung her head.

"Sit here," Themba said softly, when she was finished. He knelt down beside her. "Put your head between your legs," he instructed. "Do you want some water?"

"I'm okay," she insisted.

After a moment, he spoke. "You're right. He wasn't your relative. He did not recognize the handwriting in the notebook."

"Why?" she cried over the roar of the boat. "Why did you let me think that when you knew all along he wasn't?"

"Because," said Themba. "I think you should be open to it."

*Open to what*, Kim wanted to say. Instead she looked directly at him. "Why do you care so much if we find him?"

He did not respond to her question. "I'm going to get you a glass of water," he said, standing up.

Thank God he was gone!

Immediately Kim was ashamed. What was the matter with her? Why had she shouted at Themba?

When she opened her sticky eyes she saw Themba had returned and was standing over her. He crouched close to her. She looked into the warm brownness of his eyes.

"Maybe we're not so different after all," he said as he handed her a paper cup of water.

# TEN

# KAROO TRAIN

**K**im stretched out her legs on the top bunk, her head back against the pillow, and let the sound and motion of the train envelop her. The two-person compartment was dark, except for a small yellow sidelamp half-muted by Kim's pillow. She had no idea where they were. Somewhere en route to the Milky Way Farm.

Kim was reliving her last conversation with Themba. After the trip to Robben Island he had called her twice to make sure she was okay. She had asked Lettie to tell him she was still unwell and couldn't come to the phone. "You sick?" Lettie asked laying a warm hand on Kim's flushed cheek.

"No, I'm in seventh heaven," mumbled Kim.

But the next morning, when Themba came in person to wish her a good trip, she was relieved to see him. Her feelings toward him swung from one extreme to another. One minute she was unsure and awkward with him, the next minute, with a gesture or a word, he would put her at ease. "We need to work together if we're going to find him," he said out of earshot of Riana. "Let's go through it once more. What are you going to do at the farm?"

Kim was one step ahead of him. "I'm going to get photos, ask questions, find answers."

His face lit up. "Good. How old are your cousins?"

"The girl is fifteen, the boy fourteen."

"Perfect," said Themba. "Your cousins will let something slip, or else you'll find something – like an old diary of your ma's in the attic with a secret photo of your pa." He ran his hands over his tight wooly hair. "Who else is there?"

"My uncle, his wife, and my grandfather," Kim had said.

"Think clearly."

Kim had almost forgotten. Themba's relatives lived at the Milky Way Farm, too. Lettie's sister, for example. "Your aunt! Do you think she knows something?"

"You might have more luck with Grandma Elsie," Themba had said. "When will you be back?"

"In a week. In time for your hearing."

Themba was silent. The ex-policeman who had been involved in his father's death had applied for amnesty and the hearing was set for the end of next week. Themba was still determined not to attend, even though his mother wanted him at her side. Kim thought better of pushing the subject, and just then,

Riana's colleague, Andries, had arrived to take them to the station. While he helped Riana with her bag, Themba and Kim said their good-byes.

Cool night air whipped through the one-inch crack in the train window. Kim pulled a scratchy blanket, half wrapped in a white sheet, across her body. No doubt whatsoever, she had acted stupidly by shouting at Themba on the boat from Robben Island. But what was his problem? Why had he tried to convince her that she was related to Cape Town Harry? At times it felt like this search for her dad, her pa, as Themba called him, was a bigger deal for Themba than it was for her.

How much could she really miss having her father when she'd never known him? It was curiosity, that's all. Curiosity spurred on by the fact that her mother had sealed up the past. Still, since their arrival in South Africa, she had thought more about her father than ever before. *I need to know where I come from and who I am*, thought Kim. For one foolish second she imagined herself standing up in front of her Calgary classmates and announcing her discovery in a slick school presentation. Thanks, but no thanks.

The train suddenly slowed, jerked, and shuddered along for a minute or two, and finally came to a complete stop. Kim listened to the wheezing and sighing deep in the train's underbelly. Riana stirred in the bunk below.

Kim hoped that this trip wasn't a mistake for her mother. At the Cape Town station, shivering and pale, she'd looked like a lamb being led to slaughter. Andries hauled their bags onto the train. "Man, you exaggerate," he had chided, obviously put off by Riana's behavior.

Kim leaned on her elbows and looked out the window, her eyes probing the dark for signs of life. There was no platform, no village – only a field. Shadowy forms moved in the half-light from the train's interior. One woman had wrapped a baby on her back with a blanket.

A minute or two later, the train gathered up its strength and chugged off. Riana breathed heavily and sank deeper into sleep. Kim's thoughts returned to Themba. She had never liked a boy as much, except what a nuisance he could be! She recalled his face whenever he insisted he was right. Like the day he had told Lettie not to take herbal medicine or seek the advice of the *sangoma*. "You throw your money away on witch doctors and rubbish," he told Lettie. When Kim had tried to tell him that herbal medicine was used in Canada, he turned on her. "Kim! Kim! Herbal medicine is not the same for us as it is for you!"

Kim snapped off the yellow light. Suddenly, she could see out into the night clearly. A million bright stars embroidered a pinpoint pattern on the black sky. Cocooned by the gentle rocking of the train, Kim heard African singing, soft and melodious, like a church choir, coming from the next car.

That night Kim had a strange dream. She was seated in front of a covered wagon. Her mother lay in the back, sick with malaria, and it was Kim who drove the wagon through the empty veld. Suddenly the wagon was blocked by a circle of black youths dressed in traditional outfits. At first, Kim was surprised. Then fear took over: there were so many black youths with shields and spears. They drummed with their feet around a fire and their voices rose up into an aggressive chant as if they were preparing for an attack. One of the youths left the circle and turned to face her. It was Themba, dressed only in a leather apron with fur wrapped around his ankles.

In the morning Kim tried to shake the frightening dream from her memory. Trying not to wake her mother, she slipped into her clothes and opened the door of the compartment. In the corridor, she snapped her noisy belt buckle in place and then plunked her elbows against the ledge of the open window and leaned out as far as she could. Her feet were bare and with one foot she dragged down the bottom cuff of her jeans to stand on it rather than the cold floor of the train.

The sun had been up for hours and it was already hot. The landscape was a barren semi-desert, empty except for the odd, rightside-up pineapple bush or pile of jagged rocks – or was it an anthill? The beauty and vastness of the Karoo (her mother had promised they would wake up in the Karoo) took Kim's breath away. The sky was way too big for the land that was way too big for the sky. And there was a smell to the place! A dusty, dry, dead-leaf smell.

That smell reminded Kim of the San people displayed in the glass cases in the museum in Cape Town, their skin as yellow and dry as clay. And the image of those bushmen reminded her of Cape Town Harry. She remembered her reaction when she'd seen him and felt ashamed. Why had she rejected Cape Town Harry from the moment she laid eyes on him? It was wrong to judge people by the color of their skin, yet she had done just that. Would she judge her father the same way?

"*Koppies*," came Riana's voice from behind her. Kim was relieved that her mom had emerged from the compartment to distract her from her thoughts. She saw the black and blue hills that her mother pointed at – round forms with flat tops. Although this land, or veld as her mother called it, had once belonged to the San tribe – and to antelopes, lizards, rock-rabbits, and tortoises – today it appeared to be empty as if there was not a single human being for miles. Kim squinted. Now and then a buck or an ostrich flitted off in the distance creating small dust-clouds of life.

Riana moved slowly toward the window grasping the railing, her eyes on the veld. Then she turned to face Kim. "What do you say we have a good old-fashioned breakfast in the dining car," she said, smiling.

Riana pushed the sleeves of her blouse up past her elbows so that the full warmth from the sun could reach her skin. Her pants were rolled up to her calves like a fisherman's. Her blonde hair cascaded down her shoulders. For a moment she was the carefree mother Kim had known in Calgary.

"Let's go," Kim said not wanting to break the spell. Riana grabbed her purse and they made their way down the corridor swaying from one side to the other. "It's all exactly as I remember it," sighed Riana as they entered the dining car. The tables were covered with white linen cloths with vases of spring flowers placed on top.

"I'll have egg on toast and a chocolate milk shake," Kim said to the waiter who arrived almost immediately. "And could I please have some ketchup?" she added.

"Tomato sauce," explained Riana with a smile.

"Yes, madam," he said, as he poured Riana's coffee from a silver coffeepot. He set out two little silver pitchers: one with cold milk and the other with hot.

"It's been years since I've had anchovy toast," said Riana when the food arrived.

"When was the last time you were on a train?" Kim asked.

Riana ran her fingers through her hair. "Your *ouma* was sick and I had to go back to the farm to see her," she said after a moment.

Kim stopped drinking her chocolate shake. "I forgot about that."

Her mother looked away. "She was dying. I didn't know if I would get out to the farm in time. The train was crowded because strikes and boycotts earlier that week had disrupted travel. Hardly a bus passed that didn't have its windows smashed in. There was a particularly bad patch just outside Cape Town where trains were disrupted by school children throwing stones, because two of their classmates had been shot to death the day before by police."

Kim remembered her dream and asked, "Were you scared? Were you scared whenever you saw black people in the street?"

Riana hesitated and took a long time to answer. "Sometimes. Those were very difficult times."

Kim blurted out her question. "Was Hendrik with you on the train?" she asked.

Riana looked at her, alarmed. "No," she answered quickly. "No, he was not."

Kim pulled her straw in and out of her drink. Right here in front of her – with her espadrilles kicked off and her pant cuffs rolled up – was the one person who had all the answers. If Kim approached her carefully she just might reveal some information.

"Did your family ever meet Hendrik?" Kim asked as she drew casual circles in her milk shake.

Just as Kim feared, her mother was clamming up. For a moment, no one spoke. Kim tried another angle, but she had to go cautiously.

"You must've been scared when you found out," Kim said as she kept her straw busy inside her tall glass. "About me, I mean."

"I always wanted you," Riana said quickly. "Knowing I was pregnant made me strong," she added. "I knew *exactly* what I had to do. So often in my life, I hesitate or fluctuate or can't make up my mind. But not that time."

Kim nodded, afraid to say anything, wanting her mother to go on.

"You were like a truth drug for me," Riana continued.

"What do you mean?"

"A serum that brought out the truth. In me

and in others." Riana paused and after a moment her face stiffened. "I would prefer not to talk about it anymore."

Kim jabbed her straw against the bottom of her glass. The waiter came and took away the plates. The subject was closed – Riana had made that crystal clear. "Let's go back," she said, trying to keep her tone even. "I need to ring someone."

Kim did not budge from her chair. "Who? Andries?" Her tone was icy.

"No. I've told you a million times: Andries is just a colleague." Riana waved down the waiter. "Come. We'll be arriving soon. I'll ring my producer while you change your top."

Kim stared at her mom.

"Darling, I want them to see you in a blouse, not a T-shirt."

This suggestion floored Kim. Riana had never, not once, taken the slightest interest in what Kim wore.

"Why should I change?"

"Because I said so, I shouldn't have to explain everything over and over."

*How about explaining it just once?* thought Kim, thinking about her father. The train was slowing down and coming into a station.

"Is this it?" Kim asked, sitting up straight to see better.

"Not yet," said Riana as she exchanged money with the waiter. In her fluster Riana dropped all the change he had given her. "It's about an hour from here," she mumbled.

The train moved at a crawl. Young black children, half-dressed and shoeless, ran beside it. Kim plastered her hands against the window. Something was wrong about the way the children ran so close to the train, their pink palms open to the air. "Hey!" she said. "Are they crazy? If they get any closer they'll be run over."

"They're hungry," Riana told her as she stuffed her feet back into her espadrilles. "They're looking for food."

Only one of the children had shoes on, a long-legged girl, about Kim's age. She wore a torn dress and too-large boys' shoes. She was dragging a cart across the crowded platform. The girl took sloppy steps in her big shoes and Kim was afraid she would trip as she ran after coins tossed from the train.

Kim stood on her chair and pulled on the window with all her strength. "Open it. Quick!" she cried, pounding the window with her fists. "Mom, please, why can't we give them food?"

The waiter rushed to her side. "Come down," Riana pleaded.

"The windows are locked because of the air conditioning," said the waiter.

Kim stuffed fruit and bread from the table into her pockets. "I'm going to the door of the carriage," she said.

"No, wait," cried her mother.

Kim was about to jump down from the chair when she was frozen by what she saw on the platform. The crowd parted and there on the cart being pulled by the girl in the sloppy shoes was half a boy. Kim looked again: the boy had no legs. Using his hands, the boy gestured up at Kim.

She jumped from the chair.

"It's too dangerous," pleaded her mother. But in a second Kim was through the dining car and at the door to the next. The train lurched forward and as she forced the doors apart she cracked her elbow hard on the handle.

In the next train car, Kim paused in front of the door. Her elbow was throbbing and her eyes were spiked with tears. Holding on tightly to a bar, she flung open the outside door. No! No! No! The train was gathering speed and the platform was already gone. The last thing Kim saw was a runny-nosed dog, his ribs sticking out of his gray skin. He chased the train with all his might. Kim tossed all the food she had taken from the dining car at him.

Kim's mother was at her side, her face flushed. "I banged my elbow," Kim said, folding her knees and backing into a corner. Tears were running from her eyes as if she were a baby. She tasted their salt on her lips. "I missed them," she gasped.

Bending down beside her, Riana put an arm around her daughter. Kim fought her embrace and then relaxed into it. "Why? Why?" Kim said between sobs.

Riana held her close as the train built up speed. The sky was a dazzling blue, but through her tears Kim could see a dust storm beginning, exactly like one she had seen once on the prairies. After a while she got her breath under control. She felt calmer but her mind was filling up with more questions. "Why doesn't the new government take all the money for the Truth Commission and give it to those kids for food and a wheel chair for that boy?" she asked rubbing her sore elbow.

"I don't know," said Riana.

The conductor came by, noticed the door was open, shut it, and moved on. The motion of the train was soothing and Kim had to admit it was nice to feel her mother's arm around her.

After a while Kim spoke. "I get the feeling your family didn't approve of Hendrik," she said.

Riana nodded. "That's true."

"Maybe," Kim said as she slowly got to her feet, "they'll feel the same way about me."

# ELEVEN

# THE MILKY WAY

"The thing is this," Kim wrote to Themba the morning after they arrived at the farm, "the Van der Merwes are firmly rooted in another century – the nineteenth, I would estimate."

Kim put down her pen. She wanted to describe everything to Themba from the moment Oom Piet drove them through the high wire gate, down the gravel driveway, to the stone farmhouse with its green roof and sprawling front porch. A dozen or so people, some black and some white, had been there to greet them. Which one was Themba's grandmother, Kim had wondered. Then a stout old African woman who, the second after they climbed out of Uncle Piet's Land Rover, ambled straight over and folded her arms around Riana. Riana exclaimed with a joy Kim had rarely seen. "My Elsie," she cried, embracing her. "This is Kim."

Elsie looked Kim over with wonder. "My, my, my," she said, grinning broadly, before stepping back so the rest of the family could be introduced.

Themba's grandmother possessed Lettie's same wide body, but her skin was darker than Lettie's, the color of dark bark. Of course, Kim couldn't write that to Themba. Just like she couldn't reveal the dream she'd had of him wearing only a leather apron.

The Van der Merwes weren't going to be easy to describe either. Briefly: Kim's fair-haired, fifteen-year-old cousin, Marjike, possessed enough nail polish to open a beauty shop, yet her nails were badly bitten, some bleeding. (Her mother forbade her to wear anything but clear polish, so she nibbled at her fingers in protest.) Then there was Marjike's steely-eyed brother, Japie, who smelled of animal droppings and spent his spare time shooting small birds and burying their bones to see if fossils would form.

Not to mention Kim's long lost grandfather, Oupa. Oupa had a wiry old beard and huge, sunburnt hands. "Come," Oupa had said, ushering them into the dining room for a heavy lunch soon after they arrived.

As if in slow motion, the family crossed the slate floor, past the stone fireplace and dark, museum-like furniture of the front room toward the massive wooden dining table. The sideboard was almost as thick as the table. On top of it were oval-shaped photos of stern-faced ancestors frowning down at Kim with expressions of dislike. With the formality of church, everyone sat on throne-like chairs. "Let's bow our heads," said Oupa tugging at his steel-wool beard.

Kim shivered as Oupa gave the blessing. It seemed like the thick stone walls of the house exhaled a continuous cement-cold breath. She said her own prayer. For herself. And her mom.

"Amen," said Oupa and the food was passed. Riana, who had been a vegetarian for as long as Kim could remember, retreated about three thousand feet into herself when the joints of mutton, and the thick sausage coils were served by Elsie and her grown daughter. Kim surprised herself by enjoying the strange meats. What she did not enjoy was the way Bliksem, who in spite of his itching and drooling had been allotted the status of indoor dog, jabbed his sharp face between her knees as they sat at the lunch table.

"Our arrival at Melkweg has put everyone on edge," she continued in her letter to Themba. She thought about the best way to describe the situation. She had not been very truthful with Themba about Riana's fragile nerves and nightmares, nor had she told him that her mother was seeing a therapist. She hoped that a week away from the pressures of the Truth Commission might help her mother. However, the atmosphere at Milky Way Farm was as tense as anything Riana had faced in Cape Town. Even Oom Piet was ill at ease. Immediately after lunch, he cornered Kim in the pantry where she was looking at the rows of preserved food, some as bizarre as the pickled pig's feet in the science room back home. Piet was wearing an open-necked khaki shirt and he waved his cigarette at her. "Do you think she's going to be okay?" he demanded.

"Who?" Kim asked, watching a long line of ants swim across a saucer full of water to get to the sugar bowl.

"Your ma." Oom Piet exhaled a cloud of smoke. His face was more tanned than Kim remembered and his neck was sunburnt. "Covering this commission – it's not a job for a lady, *nê*?" He stubbed out his cigarette on the bottom of his boot.

*Not if a lady is someone like your wife*, Kim thought. Her Aunt Reza was like a character right out of a Halloween thriller. Clad in a black dress, black stockings and shoes, and prone to monster headaches, Tante Reza either locked herself up in the attic all day, or sat silently on the porch drinking tea, waving the flies off her face with an ostrich feather.

Better to write to Themba about the outdoor dogs – half a dozen of them – with their hot breath and dancing tails, and the elegant horses, Willem and Tara, who neighed and pranced in the fields around the house. Kim especially loved the guinea fowl that ran wild on the farm. They had miniature white polka dots and the funniest looking crimson-red headpieces above their bright blue necks. Cute, but would Themba care?

Kim put down her pen and glanced across the room at Marjike's empty bed. Before they had gone to sleep, Marjike had produced about six different kinds of pimple cream. "Pimple cream for Africa," she joked as she smeared the most fluorescent brand across her chin. "Ma would have a fit. Ma thinks pimples is, I mean are, a result of standing too long in front of the mirror."

Kim rolled her head back on the stiff pillow. What a bizarre place – a farm named after the Milky Way – her mother's girlhood home. But it was beautiful too. The Cape winter had been cold and rainy, but green. By contrast, the landscape around the farm was dry and dusty – more African – and beautiful in a way that she couldn't begin to put down on paper.

Kim turned back to her letter. She knew that what Themba would really want to hear were clues about her father. And she had none. In addition, she was beginning to realize that it would not be easy to get her relatives to open up.

A minute later, Marjike was standing over Kim with a tray of hot coffee and a bowl full of rusks. "*Koffie en beskuit*," Marjike announced. "Japie says I must practice being more ladylike," she said, as she poured out the milky coffee.

Kim had never been served food in bed before. A round lacy cloth with tiny pink shells dangling from the edge, covered the sugar bowl. "These are called babies' toes," Marjike said, as she fingered the fat little shells.

Then her cousin looked at the envelop beside Kim's bed. "Who are you writing to?" she asked. "A boy or a girl?"

Kim found the coffee too hot and bitter to drink. "A guy, you know, in my class," she explained, carefully setting the cup back on the tray. "When I finish will you help me mail this?"

Marjike's eyes widened as she checked Themba's last name on the envelope. "We will send the letter to town with our garden boy. But don't tell Japie that you have an African friend." Marjike chewed on her fingers and added, "You're lucky you don't have a brother. Last month I bought myself a Foschini backless halter. Japie cut it up with scissors for a rabbit bed. . . . Something wrong, Kim?"

"No," Kim said through clenched teeth. She wasn't about to tell her cousin what she could do with her brother.

Just before breakfast, Kim ran into her mother out on the porch. Except for the hyperactive outdoor dogs that guarded the house, Kim and her mother were alone.

"We should have brought Themba with us," said Kim. "So he could see his grandmother."

"Oupa would not have allowed it," Riana said in a dull voice. She looked as if she hadn't slept.

"In thirteen years, haven't they changed at all?" Kim asked.

"I don't know," muttered Riana.

At that moment Elsie's daughter, wearing a blue uniform and a blue headscarf around her head, announced that breakfast was served. The family congregated around the enormous yellowwood table in the kitchen. All through the meal, Kim kept her eye on her cousin Japie. He loved to jab his rusk into his black coffee and then scatter the gooey crumbs across the table before plunging the rusk into his mouth. While Tante Reza passed eggs and sausage she ignored her piggy son, yet watched Kim's manners and the placement of her elbows with a sharp eye. "Does Oupa want some more milk?" she asked in a baby voice as Elsie's daughter arrived with a pitcher of boiled milk. With a sinking heart, Kim realized that getting information out of these people would be like communicating with rocks.

Suddenly, as they finished up breakfast, a vehicle charged up the farm road at a terrific speed. Uncle Piet jumped to his feet and went to the back door to quiet the dogs. Japie left the room and returned with a rifle. Tante Reza glanced nervously from the door to Riana and spoke. "When a car turns up at the gate, we don't know if it's *vriend of vyand*. Friend or enemy."

Oupa dropped his fork and tried to stand.

"Oupa, sit," Piet said, as Japie put down the rifle. "It's just Old Koos. He's in a new vehicle."

The neighbor was in a hurry and would not stay. Marjike translated it all for Kim. "Someone is stealing his cattle. When he finds out who it is, he will set the dogs on them," Marjike added as she poured out more coffee. "If that doesn't work he'll shoot them."

"Must I bring Pa's other rifle?" asked Japie.

"Bring it!" Uncle Piet told him.

Kim glanced across at her mom with concern.

"It's just routine," explained her uncle. "We need to patrol the land."

"I'm going to show Kim the horses," announced Marjike, as she got up from the table. "Fix your hair first," Tante Reza said looking at both her daughter and Kim before she left the kitchen and headed for the wooden staircase on the outside of the farmhouse.

Kim watched her aunt slowly climb the stairs that led up to the attic. What would it be like to be the daughter of a crazy mother? Kim might be in that position herself, if Riana wasn't back on a plane to Canada in three weeks as planned. Kim pulled back her hair with the thick vegetable elastic she kept in her pocket for when it became too frizzy. Then Oom Piet appeared in the doorway with two rifles.

"This is ridiculous!" cried Riana. "If there's trouble you should phone the police. You don't take matters into your own hands."

Uncle Piet was feeling for his cigarettes. "Forget calling the police," he said. He exhaled heavily. "They're in league with the thieves now."

Kim looked anxiously from her uncle to her mother. Would it be safe for Marjike and her to leave the farmhouse?

Riana got up abruptly from the table. "Nothing's changed," she snapped.

"My girl, you've got that right," Oom Piet said, slamming the door as he left.

# TWELVE

# A RIGHT TO KNOW

"**W**hat is she saying?" asked Kim. It was very obvious to Kim that Elsie's daughter, Rosie, was talking about her. As soon as Oom Piet had gone off with the neighbor and Marjike had gone to her room to fix her hair, Rosie had padded out with a large tray and begun to clear the table. Suddenly, she stopped what she was doing, stared across at Kim, and said something to Riana in Afrikaans.

"Nothing," said her mother, rubbing her lips together. Riana had announced that she had a story to work on, but instead of bolting away from the table, she sank deeper into her chair.

Rosie clicked her tongue against the side of her cheek, exactly like Lettie might have done, and continued speaking.

"She's talking about me," insisted Kim to her mother.

Riana leaned forward. She was stroking the table like it was a long lost friend. "Look, Rosie, how you've kept it polished up," she muttered.

"Mother!" Kim said.

"She says you remind her of her oldest daughter," Riana explained. "She is your age and she is away at school."

Kim was about to question how she with her long unruly hair could look anything like the cropped-haired, chocolate-skinned Rosie. But before she could say anything a voice came from the first door off the kitchen. Kim peered inside, heard her name, and took a few steps forward.

When Kim's eyes adjusted to the dim light she saw that the room was filled with rows of books in high glass bookcases. In front of her, sitting on an antique desk, was an old-fashioned Bible, bound in leather. Suddenly she heard the sharp strike of a matchstick and wheeled around. It was Oupa, her grandfather, lighting his pipe with a long match. Behind him, in a glass case, were three large guns.

Kim moved closer to inspect them. "Can you shoot those? I mean do they still work?" she asked.

"We all shoot," explained Oupa in careful English. His voice was raspy and uneven. "Except your mother. She refused to learn to shoot a gun." Oupa and Kim listened as Riana and Rosie laughed together in the kitchen. Then he pointed to an oval frame on the wall. "Riana takes after her great-ouma, her great-grandmother, as you say."

Oupa sucked on his pipe as Kim looked at the portrait. The woman had a high lace collar and the man beside her, a dark Sunday-best suit. The man clenched a long gun in one hand.

"Her husband, Marthinus van der Merwe, fought and survived the Zulu wars up North," he explained. "They had six sons before Great-Ouma was bitten by a snake. Great-Ouma survived a British concentration camp only to come home and be killed by a snake. Why? Because she did not know how to shoot."

Kim wanted to know more about snakes – and what to do if she saw one – but she decided to ask something else instead. She needed something to tell Themba, and she was getting impatient. She decided to jump in with her question. "Oupa," she began boldly. "Did my father know how to shoot?"

Her grandfather's forehead furrowed. "I wouldn't know that," he responded.

Kim heart was thumping. "Did you ever meet Hendrik?" she asked.

Oupa's pipe had gone out and he knocked the ash from it before responding. "I met him once," he said. "He had come up here to the farm from Cape Town to see your ma. He came up in secret, and Lettie hid him in her room in the compound."

"Lettie?" Kim asked, trying to keep her voice steady. She wasn't sure she had heard her grandfather correctly. "The woman who works for us in Cape Town?"

"Ja," Oupa said. He fumbled for a pipe cleaner and said in an earnest voice: "You must pass my words onto her. You must tell Lettie I am very sorry for the fire and for all that happened during that time."

*What fire?* thought Kim. She also wondered what Hendrik was hiding from. But before she could ask Oupa these questions, he pointed the end of his pipe cleaner at a photo in a plastic frame. "Do you not recognize your Oom Piet?" he asked. Kim looked closer. There was a photo of a blond youth in an army uniform with a bunch of soldiers on top of an armored tank.

"I think that was taken in Transvaal," he said twisting the pipe cleaner inside his pipe.

There was a wedding photo of Oom Piet and Tante Reza and then three photos of babies. Kim stopped in her tracks. Who was the third child?

Oupa moved her along, obviously not wanting her to ask about the baby photos. He listened to make sure Riana was still occupied with Rosie and then asked: "How is your ma's life over there in Canada?"

Kim hesitated. It was hard to change gears so quickly and think about home.

"Your mom has her courage," Oupa said, refilling his pipe. "But it is a life of loneliness, nê? No nation. No roots. No tribe."

What an odd way to sum up Riana's life. Riana's life in Canada was pretty good, and as far as Kim was concerned, she was counting the days until they would be back there.

Marjike poked her head into the study and Oupa indicated that Kim should follow her. They said good-bye and made their way to the back porch. Kim surveyed the farm from there, listened for gunshots, and wondered out loud if it was safe to leave the house.

"The wire fence is electric," explained Marjike. "It protects the house, the barn, and the outbuildings from intruders."

Kim watched as Elsie and Rosie hauled two large pots of soup for the workers who had come especially to dig a swimming pool.

"Oupa said we could finally have one," said Marjike excitedly as they watched dozens of blue-overalled men overturn the soil with shovels and picks. "For years and years we fought with Oupa about the pool. He would not allow it."

"How come?"

"Oupa said we were too young. He did not want any child to have an accident in it."

Kim remembered the third baby in the photo and wondered when might be a good time to ask Marjike about the child. As they crossed the field to the barn, she saw six of Bliksem's relatives sleeping in a sloppy pile against a brick wall. Kim looked around for her favorite birds. There they were, her guinea fowl, resting under the rhubarb patch. They came out to greet her.

"Pa doesn't want you to ride yet," said Marjike as she slid open the barn door. "Why not?" asked Kim.

"He wants to make sure there are no accidents," explained her cousin.

*Why is this family so slaphappy with guns, yet so scared of accidents?* Kim thought, as she entered the barn. Two horses, standing in box stalls, towered over her. She watched Marjike pick up a large thick sponge and step right into the stall with the largest horse.

"It works like this, see," said Marjike, pulling the horse's face close to her. "To groom the horses I begin at Willem's ears and brush in the direction of the hairs." Cautiously, Kim moved closer to Willem. He was a large red horse with fast-blinking eyes and a black mane. "Now you try," Marjike said, holding Willem tightly.

*Shooz!* The barn door whirled open just as Kim began brushing Willem. The noise caused the animal to start and almost step on Kim's foot. Great! It was Japie.

Marjike frowned and said, "I thought you were helping Pa." Japie stood in the doorway with one hand on his hip. In his other hand was a red, ball-shaped fruit – a split-open pomegranate.

"Just ignore him," instructed Marjike as she turned back to the horse. "Try with Tara. She's gentle." As Kim approached the fair horse in the next stall, she could feel Japie's eyes burning into her. What was his problem anyway? She got the distinct feeling that Japie hated her guts.

"It's okay," reassured Marjike. "She can't kick with the front leg."

Marjike showed her how to run her hand down the back of the leg and grab the foot by holding the front of the hoof. She had a little pick in her hand. "Wiggle the hoof pick in there," Marjike explained. "Scrape out mud, stones, the works."

Kim was sweating. If only they could finish grooming the horses and just ride them.

"Watch out," shouted Japie, spitting the pomegranate pips to the ground. "She's hurting Tara. Look!"

"Mind your own business," yelled Marjike to her brother. She turned to Kim. "Careful around the spongy area of her hoof."

Kim did as she was told and then put Tara's foot down.

"Come. Let's walk them around a bit," suggested Marjike. "You lead Tara and I'll take Willem."

Japie tossed down the half-eaten piece of pomegranate. "I hope you both get rabies from a meerkat," he said.

As Kim guided Tara outside, she heard the roar of an engine. She turned to see Japie jump on his dirt bike, point it into the path of her favorite guinea fowl, and speed off behind a row of aloe trees. The lovely birds were sent scrambling for cover behind the barn.

What was his problem? The only thing to do was ignore the creep. As she glanced in the direction where the birds had taken shelter, she noticed a row of old shacks. She hadn't seen these before. Most of the walls had crumbled in and there was only the framework and roofs in place.

"What are those?" Kim asked.

"Only ants live there now," said Marjike. "The compound burned down about the time your ma left for Canada. Elsie and her family used to live there. Now they live in new rooms up closer to the house."

Kim remembered how Oupa had asked her to tell Lettie he was sorry about the fire. She wondered again why Hendrik would have been hiding in Lettie's room. "Did Oupa burn down their rooms?" Kim asked.

Marjike shrugged. "Oupa had an accident and a fire began." Kim waited for something else, but that was all her cousin would reveal. She watched Marjike pull herself easily up onto Willem's back. "I'm going to let Willem run. You can walk Tara around the yard, but do not ride her. Stay close to

the house. And don't go near the fence that sur-
rounds the *werf*."

"What's a werf?" asked Kim.

"It's the open area around the yard," Marjike
explained. "Careful. Remember the wire fence is
turned on."

Keeping far away from the fence, Kim led Tara
on the path beside the farmhouse. Rosie was fetching
some firewood at the side of the house. The workers'
picks thumped as they dug out the new pool.

Suddenly, Kim heard angry voices coming
from the kitchen. Piet and her mother were arguing.

Kim tied Tara up to a tree and drew closer to
the kitchen window. She glanced over her shoulder;
Marjike couldn't see her. She was riding Willem in
the open field beyond the barn and the electric
fence. Kim snuck closer. Rosie wouldn't notice; she
was occupied with the firewood.

Kim leaned in to the open window. She
couldn't believe her eyes. Her mother had gone
through Kim's photos from Canada and had them
spread all over the yellowwood table. Flushed, Riana
was banging her fists against the heavy table. Whatever point she was making to Uncle Piet and Oupa,
Riana was going about it too hard.

Kim strained to hear the conversation. What was
going on? How dare her mother go through her stuff!

"Does Pa think it was easy for me?" lashed out

Riana, screaming in English. "Me, alone in a new country with a baby! I showed you these pictures so you could see how hard our life was."

"What Pa is saying, is . . ." said Piet reaching for a cigarette, ". . . you were the one who left for a safer land. The rest of us had to steel ourselves to stay in Africa."

Oupa shook his head angrily. Riana's face was distorted with fury. Oom Piet stepped back to give her some breathing room.

"Just leave it now, Riana," he continued. "You too, Pa. Let it go."

Kim had to get away before someone saw her. But she could not move an inch until Rosie was out of sight.

Now Oupa was shouting. It was a side of her grandfather that Kim hadn't yet seen. "She has been asking questions about her father!" His beard was within an inch of Riana's face.

Rosie disappeared into the house with the firewood. Kim, just in the nick of time, crawled away from the window. Untangling Tara's reins from the tree, Kim led the horse quickly away from the house. But not before she heard her grandfather say: "She has a right to know!"

# THIRTEEN

# THE ARK

"Have you been to his house in the township?" Marjike asked Kim over her shoulder. "Your friend Themba's?"

Both girls were sitting on the grand red horse, Willem. Marjike had on riding breeches, tall boots, and her hair was braided into a plait. Kim wore jeans and a pair of old boots Marjike had lent to her. Out of view of the farmhouse, they were ambling in the field on the other side of the electric fence. Kim watched how Marjike communicated with Willem using her entire body, adjusting his speed with a single word or a pull to the rein.

"Yeah, I've been to his place," Kim answered. She rested one arm on Marjike's waist, the other hand held the reins for Tara who was following behind them. "He eats the same thing for breakfast as we do, you know," Kim added, imagining how Themba would laugh when she shared this conversation with him later. Ever since Marjike had helped Kim mail Themba's letter, five days ago, there had been a series of questions about him.

"The only Blacks I ever meet are laborers," said Marjike as they guided Willem and Tara around a row of old pepper trees.

*Slaves is more like it,* thought Kim, recalling the swimming-pool men and poor Elsie and her over-worked daughter. But she didn't say it. The truth was, Kim had thoroughly enjoyed her time on the farm and didn't mind one bit having people wait on her hand and foot.

During the five days she had spent at Milky Way, Kim had fallen easily into the rhythms of life in the country. People woke very early and smoke drifted in from the workers' houses so it was the first thing you smelled when you stepped on the back porch. Kim would sit for a long time on the stoep listening to the wooing bird noises and watching the sun push up into the wide, empty, African sky. Sometimes Bliksem would join her, sprawling at her feet instead of doing his job of pacing around the farmyard and keeping snakes and other creatures away. Each morning there was a big breakfast, after which Marjike and Kim would take the horses past the fence and into the vast fields beyond the farmhouse.

Even though she had enjoyed the farm, Kim was well aware that since the morning she had overheard the argument with her mom and grand-father, she had found out nothing new to report to Themba. Cornering her mother was impossible. As luck would have it, a nearby town was a site for one of the Truth and Reconciliation Commission hearings and suddenly, Riana was bombarded with work for her radio station. *What we need is a Truth Commission in this family*, thought Kim.

Kim pulled on Tara's rein urging the mare to keep up. Over the last five days Kim had been mainly with her cousin, learning how to ride. It was kind of Marjike to teach her, but Kim was frustrated that she was not allowed to ride solo on her own horse. That was why Tara had to trail behind them. Tara's big questioning eyes mirrored Kim's: *How long before we have the chance to ride together?*

After a while Marjike slowed the horses and let them drop their heads in a tussock of low grass. She pointed to a ruin made out of baked clay and stone. One wall rose a few feet from the ground, the rest had dissolved away. Two small lizards wiggled away from the ruins and into the dust. "That's our great-great-grandparents' homestead," she told Kim. The use of the word *our* sounded odd to Kim, yet nice. She wondered what it would be like to have Marjike for a sister.

Behind the remains of the homestead were rows of old gravestones surrounded by a low whitewashed wall. On one side, beside a crooked thorn tree, was a newer grave with a small marker.

Kim leaned forward. On the tombstone there

was a small image of a baby chiseled into it. "Who's that?" Kim asked.

"Katie. My little sister," said Marjike.

"I didn't know you had a sister."

"Check this out." Marjike pointed at a beetle moving slowly across the ground. "It is a dung beetle. Do you know what dung is?"

"No," said Kim. She wanted to ask more about the baby but didn't know how.

"Dung is poo hey," said Marjike and then added, "Katie died when I was three."

Kim wasn't sure what to say. In silence they watched as the stout beetle slowly, painstakingly rolled a ball of brown goo three or four sizes bigger than itself. Suddenly Marjike pulled back hard on the reins. "Oh no!" she cried. "The baboons are at our fig trees."

Off in the distance Kim could see a family of baboons surrounding a patch of trees. They were pulling down the figs and stuffing as many as they could into their mouths. One mother had a baby hanging upside down from her stomach; another had a youngster riding piggyback.

This was great. Kim had never seen a baboon out of a zoo. "They're so cute!"

"They're beasts," cried Marjike. "And they're dangerous! The big males can tear out a dog's stomach. Hold on."

Kim coiled her arms tighter around Marjike's waist as the horses took off. "*Voertsek!*" Marjike shouted as they gained speed. Kim closed her eyes.

When she dared to look, Kim saw the baboons scattering. They tried to carry off as many figs as possible, some under their armpits, some in their hands. As they ran the fruit flew all over the place.

The last thing she saw was a male baboon lifting his dog-snout face to survey the scene before he disappeared over a small hill. Marjike bent over to reward Willem with some pats on the side of his neck. Kim relaxed her grip on Marjike's waist. It was a cool day and the blue sky was broken up with large dark clouds that rolled in over the mountains.

Marjike pointed off in the distance, "Look. There's Oupa's ship. His Noah's Ark."

"It's as big as a house!" exclaimed Kim. It was Noah's Ark, all right, resting high and mighty up on wooden stilts. The bottom of the boat was massive and sloped away from a tall mast and a stout, red-painted cabin. Behind the wondrous craft the land spread out dry and golden for miles.

Marjike steered the horses in the direction of the ark. "Oupa named it from an etching he saw as a child in a children's Bible," she explained. "Oupa had no knowledge of boats. I'm not lying if I tell you the poor old ark has never once seen a lake or an ocean."

"Can we go inside?"

Marjike nodded and they tied the horses to a thorn tree beside the tall wooden ladder that led from the ground to the hull. Then they saw the dirt bikes. "Japie and his friends are here," Marjike said with some concern.

"I don't care," said Kim. "Let's climb up." Both her hands and her feet were already on the ladder.

"Be careful," cautioned Marjike. "Don't look down, man. It's much higher than it seems."

Kim soon realized what Marjike meant. Halfway up she made the mistake of dropping her eyes. The golden ground swam below her and her legs began to shake. She focused on the top of the ladder and forced herself to keep going. Finally, she stepped over a wooden rail, onto the deck of the boat.

"What are they doing in there?" Kim whispered the moment Marjike was safely beside her.

"Hey," warned Marjike. "Sh!"

Kim looked around. The ship had curved wooden sides that swept up much higher than her head. Oupa had made counters and some wooden seats under a carving of a sea bird. It was weird to be walking on an ark suspended high above land.

"Listen," whispered Marjike. "I think they're downstairs in the hold."

Kim could hear mumbled sounds from the bottom of the ark. It sounded like the boys were giggling, or tumbling, or perhaps fighting. The two cousins stepped quietly across the wooden deck.

Kim arrived first at the hatch that led down into the hold where cargo would be kept. The ship vibrated with each thud and wham. Three or four candles flickered and it took a moment for Kim's eyes to distinguish what she saw. Down below her, Japie and a carrot-topped friend were wrestling each other with pillows.

Some secret meeting. One of the pillows had burst and feathers flew like fairies through the air and all over the boys.

Japie was the first to see the girls. "*Wat kyk hulle!*" he barked. He batted the feathers away, furious. He looked silly.

"Way to go," Kim said.

"*Voertsek!*" he shouted the same word Marjike had used to chase away the baboons.

"Let's go," said Marjike, pulling Kim away.

"*Foot-sack* yourself," said Kim.

Japie frowned. "She's the cousin I told you about," he told his pal. The boy was a hillbilly with orange hair and orange eyelashes. His skin was translucent as if he never came into the sun, and his trousers were worn at the knees. "She's the one whose ma had to take off to Canada." Jap's voice echoed in the hollow hull of the boat.

Marjike went very still. "Japie, shut up," she said.

"I knew it, man," said the hillbilly boy. He was out of breath from the pillow fight and the corners of his mouth glistened with saliva. "The minute she walked in here, I knew it."

Kim flushed. "Knew what?" she demanded, planting her hands on her hips.

"Her pa was colored all right," said Japie, spitting onto the floor. "If you know what to look for," he added with a knowing grin, "you can see it a mile off."

Kim pulled herself up as if to shout back, but no words came to her lips. Instead, she turned and marched away. In two seconds she was past the wooden seats and back at the place where the ladder rested against the side of the ship. Her heart was beating like crazy as she heard Marjike scolding the boys. "Tell her you're sorry, hey," she said.

"I'm *not* sorry," echoed Japie's voice.

Climbing down was much harder than climbing up. If Kim missed a rung she could fall to her death. She wanted to get as far away as possible. She started down – one rung at a time – holding the sides tightly, forcing herself to go slowly. It felt like an eternity before she was at the bottom of the long ladder. Without hesitating, she untied Willem's reins and hauled herself up onto his back.

Willem lifted his head and looked at Kim with bright, questioning eyes. Kim gathered up the reins and gave him a quick hard kick as she had seen Marjike do. Willem obeyed. Leaving Tara tied to the thorn tree, he bolted.

Kim tried to focus on what she was doing. Except she was not riding Willem; the horse had taken control. He was going way too fast. *Stop*, she tried to shout, but her voice was frozen with fear. *Please stop!* Kim's entire body jarred with every stride.

She had to gain control or Willem would kill them both. That realization, coupled with her anger, helped her to overcome her fear. She pulled smoothly back on the reins. Show the horse who is boss, Marjike had taught her. Miraculously, the horse obeyed. Willem calmed down and galloped smoothly and evenly. She was doing it. She was riding Willem! And she didn't stop, didn't need to stop, until they were way out in the middle of the veld, in the middle of nowhere, where the scent grew stronger and spicier and the dust redder and dryer and there was nothing around them but silence.

"Whoa," she called to Willem, pulling back on the reins. He slowed to a trot, then came to a stop, his sides heaving. Kim stroked his neck. "Good boy," she told him, amazed that her voice still worked, even though her hands were shaking.

She shivered and pulled herself closer to the hot body of the horse. Her hair had come out of its elastic and now it fell across Willem's mane. A memory flooded back to Kim. "Horsehair," a kid had once called her. When had that happened? She had been seven or eight and there was a fight over it, maybe even her first fist fight.

The sun had gone under a dark cloud, leaving little light except on the distant purple mountains. A rust-brown bird with a long beak landed on a nearby bush. It's repeated cry – *tjip-tjip-tjippie-e* – brought her back to attention. The sky was very dark. It would rain – soon.

Kim gathered up the reins. She should never have let those stupid boys get to her. It was Riana's fault that she had run away from Japie like an idiot. What was Riana's problem? Why had she kept the truth about her father a secret? Was she ashamed of the very blood that ran through Kim's veins?

A large raindrop splattered on her hand, then another hit the back of her neck. *Riana is going to tell me the truth once and for all! She is going to set this straight today!* Kim took up the reins, and, kicking her heels into Willem's flanks, sent him galloping through the rain in the direction of the farmhouse.

# FOURTEEN

# THE PENCIL TEST

The rain came down in sheets. Kim had just gotten Willem into the barn and thrown a blanket over him when the thunder exploded. Through the open door of the barn, lightning flickered and turned everything white – one, two, three, four flashes in a row and then darkness. Even though Willem must be used to such African storms, he was spooked. He squealed and backed into the corner of his stall.

Kim dashed for the farmhouse and burst into darkness. For a moment she didn't understand what was going on. There was a paraffin lantern flickering on the center of the yellowwood table. Rosie was down on her hands and knees building a fire in the front-room stone fireplace. "The electricity is broken," said Rosie when she saw Kim's face.

Tante Reza, dressed in coffin black and carrying a candle, shuffled out of the dark toward Kim. "Japie and Marjike called me on the cell phone," she said. "They are still in the boat. They are taking cover there from the storm."

Suddenly Kim noticed the handle of a gun peeking out of Tante Reza's dress pocket. Terrified, she took a step back. "Where's my mom?" she demanded staring at the gun. Her clothes were drenched and her wet hair was clinging to her shoulders.

"Your Oom Piet took her to the train station."

"Train station?"

"Ja, the newspaper or the radio, I don't know which, sent a message and asked your mother to go to Lion's River to cover some story," Tante Reza said.

"What story?" Kim asked.

"I don't know. She left this note for you." Tante Reza handed her an envelope. "Must I ask Elsie to make you some tea?"

"No," said Kim.

"Take this candle please," her aunt instructed. "You must change your clothes."

Kim hesitated before taking the candle: her hands were shaking and she thought the candle would roll out of its holder and burn her skin. But she did as she was told and, taking the note and candle with her, made her way to the back of the house.

When she reached Marjike's room, she set the brass candlestick on the dresser, slammed the door, and flung herself on the second bed in her soaked clothes. She couldn't stand it. She couldn't stand being left in the dark in this spooky farmhouse with a certifiable nutcase at the one time she needed her mom the most. Kim made a fist and pounded the bed until the candlelight flickered across the walls and her hand began to throb.

She ripped open the letter and held it close to the candle. "*My darling Kim*," it began. How incredibly fake. Just like her mom to try and butter her up and then run off in the middle of a storm and abandon her.

"*I have to go to a nearby town to cover a story for my producer. There have been some protests about the Truth Hearings going on there this week. When the commission descended on this small town they underestimated the anger that people feel. I should be back in a couple of days.*"

A couple of days! Kim pounded the bed again. Her mother had promised this would be a holiday. Didn't her boss at the radio station understand what he was putting her mother through? He couldn't go on making her cover stories about dead babies, tortured teenagers, and bomb blasts so deadly that roofs were blown off. Kim turned back to the letter.

"*Please try and be patient. I know this has not been an easy time. So much has been kept secret and it is very frustrating for you. I promise I will reveal everything soon. Be good to Tannie Reza, Oom Piet, and Oupa.*
*With love, your mother.*"

Kim tossed the letter to the ground and started, as a clap of thunder boomed outside the farmhouse.

What a pathetic letter! A million questions tumbled through her mind and this stupid letter added even more.

There was a knock on the door.

For a split second Kim thought it was her mother returning early from the story. But no doubt it was stern-faced Tante Reza with a "please Kim" expression on her face and a hand gun in her apron.

Kim flung open the door and was astonished to see her grandfather standing there with a tray of tea and a second candle. Silently, she watched Oupa stoop and set the tray down on the dressing table. His chest was sunken and every hair on his head was snow-white, even his eyebrows. He set the candle on the other side of the dresser and closed the curtains.

"I heard you and my mom fighting the other day," Kim cried. "Is that why she left?"

Oupa awkwardly shifted his weight from one foot to the other. "Your ma is stubborn and so is your Oupa. A few days ago we did have an argument, but we made up. Your ma went away for her work and will soon return."

Kim looked as if she did not believe him. Oupa leaned forward and removed something from his trouser pocket. "This was Great-Ouma's brooch," he said as he put a silver pin set with a dark red stone into Kim's hand. "Your great-ouma grew up so quiet she was almost mute," he added. "She was forbidden to speak her mother tongue, Afrikaans. The British made her wear an 'I am a donkey' sign and take a beating if she tried to speak Afrikaans in school."

Kim did not know what to say. She cradled the heavy brooch in her palms. "Ouma would have liked you to have it." Oupa was about to leave the room when he paused at the door. "Did you see the graves of our ancestors?" he asked.

*Our ancestors?* What was he talking about? Then she remembered the graveyard Marjike had shown her.

"I saw them," Kim said. She did not want him to leave. She had so much to ask him. "I saw all the graves, Oupa," she added as she ran her finger across the glowing stone.

Oupa held up all his old twisted fingers, then made two fists, and folded out three more fingers, so Kim could count how many generations of Van der Merwes had been in Africa. Thirteen. That was a lot. But what about Themba? What was he? The thousandth generation? Maybe more.

*I saw Lettie's old house*, Kim almost blurted, but something stopped her. *I saw how Lettie's old house had been burned.*

Oupa rubbed his fingers through his disheveled hair as if he could hear her silent accusations. He even looked as if he was about to add something else when Tante Reza beckoned him. Again, he made for the door. "Please. Now you must rest," he said before shutting it quietly behind him.

Frustrated, Kim tossed the brooch down onto the bed. She remembered the phone on Marjike's dresser, fumbled for the receiver, and tapped out Themba's number by the light of the candle. It was late afternoon – Themba might be in the township, he might not.

He picked the phone up himself. "Kim? Kim, I am happy to hear from you," he said in his distinct voice. "How are you enjoying your holiday?" He spoke exactly as if she was off on a picnic.

Kim had trouble keeping her voice steady. "Fine, Themba, yes, just – fine. Perfect." Receiver to her ear, she sat on the bed and began to thump the place where she made a hollow in the mattress. Her jerky shadow jumped on the walls around her.

"How's it man?" Themba asked. "You sound out of breath."

Kim tried to calm herself. "I sort of stole a horse, if you want to know the truth."

"*Hau*, Kim! Are you becoming a criminal now?" His deep belly laugh rumbled in her ear. "If so, I would suggest that –"

Kim struggled to keep her voice light. "Just hold back on the expert advice for once," she joked, though she didn't feel at all like joking.

The lightning blinked through the closed curtains. Kim picked up the brooch from the bed and stuffed it into her jeans pocket.

"Tell me what you have found out about your father," Themba said. "What have they told you?"

"My cousin told me the truth," Kim said. "Except my mom has gone off to Lion's River and isn't here to confirm it."

"Then I'll tell you what I know," Themba began after a moment. "I received your letter yesterday. When you described the burned-down compound, abandoned to the wind and the ants, I figured that there was more to it. I wondered if my ma might know something. When I questioned her, sure enough. She knew Hendrik."

Kim swallowed. "Go on."

"'Colored' is how your father would have been classified in the old South Africa," continued Themba. "He dated your mom while they attended University of Cape Town, one of the few universities he could attend. One night he traveled from Cape Town to the farm to find your ma. Hendrik and Riana had had a serious argument about what to do once they found out your mom was pregnant. He came to the farm to find her and it was my ma who hid him in her room in the compound."

Kim caught her breath. The rain beat hard on the tin roof of the farmhouse. She pressed the receiver close to her ear to hear better. Themba added, "Ma sheltered Hendrik for three days in her room while your mom visited him secretly so they could talk. Your grandfather found out and in a fit of temper he burned down the rooms and banished Ma from the farm forever. Grandma Elsie wailed for forgiveness, but there was no changing your grandfather's heart. This is the reason Ma has never returned to the farm since."

The line went silent. After a moment Themba spoke. "Are you okay?"

"Yes." Kim's voice was almost inaudible.

"And the news about your father. Are you in a good shock or a bad one?" he added, letting his voice lift.

Kim didn't know what to think. If her mother and others saw her father as a dirty secret, then what was she? Her words came in a rush. "She was ashamed of my father! That's why she never told me!"

"Calm down," Themba cautioned. "I can only hear about every second word. Your connection is breaking down."

"We're having a storm." She turned in the opposite direction. "Is that better?" She was speaking as loud as she dared. She didn't want her aunt to know she was on the phone.

"Ja, listen," he said. "You don't understand. You must see it from your ma's side."

Was he defending her mother? Had he gone crazy?

"I'm going to give you an example," he said. "They did this test. They did something called the pencil test. Can you hear me?"

"Yes, I can."

"A chap I play soccer with told me about his older brother," Themba said. "He was much lighter than the entire family. It was unbelievable how light-skinned he was. A Greek god, his mother called him. When he was six she had a plan – to pass him off as white. You know, so he could go to the white school and get a better education. At school, the first week, the authorities put a pencil into his hair, to see if the pencil would stick in or fall out. He failed the test, Kim."

She stood up, took two steps to the desk, and picked up an orange pencil from a jar where Marjike kept them. She stood in front of the oval mirror on the wall.

"Think, man," Themba continued, "if they found out your pa was colored. You would not have been able to live where your mother lived. Or go to a white hospital if you were sick. Your whole life would have been controlled. Controlled by them."

What was she doing? Her face in the mirror was distorted by candlelight as she lifted the pencil to her hair.

"Are you there?" Themba asked.

"Yes."

She heard him take a deep breath.

"Kim, you're six years old, the first day of school, you fail the pencil test. *Think!* You would have been chased out of the white school like a dog!"

The orange pencil stuck fast in her hair. Even as she moved her head, the pencil did not roll out from the place where she had jabbed it in.

"Kim?"

She swallowed but did not answer. From the window she could see the bright lights of Oom Piet's Land Rover coming up the laneway. The storm had suddenly stopped.

"Themba," she said yanking the pencil from her hair. "I gotta go."

She slammed down the receiver and rushed down the stairs to meet her uncle.

# FIFTEEN

# FIRE

"I have to see my mom," Kim said the minute Oom Piet walked into the kitchen.

"Too late, my girl. She's already left for Lion's River."

"Just drop me off at the train station then," she pleaded. "I can take the train from there."

Oom Piet frowned and lit a cigarette. He walked through the dark house into the front rooms. "My girl, forget about that."

Kim followed her uncle. "Why not?"

He coiled his arm around her. "To start with, it's not safe. Besides you need more than just a train trip to get to where your ma is. Lion's River is over an hour's drive from here." Kim stood still. His arm around her made her feel stiff as a board.

"Please. The storm has stopped," Kim pleaded.

Piet tried to reassure her about her mother, but Kim wasn't convinced. Especially when she found out that Riana had been called away to cover a fire burning out of control.

"Fire?" shouted Kim. "Nobody said anything about a fire!"

"The fire was set in protest of the commission," explained Oom Piet. "Some of the locals do not want the Truth Hearings in their town." Her uncle looked at her face and hastened to add. "She's perfectly safe and away from where the fire is. So, please don't worry. I'm going out there myself. The fire is threatening homes on the outskirts of the town – far from where your ma is – and they need men to divert it."

"*Divert* it!" yelled Kim. "Why not put it out?"

"That's what I mean," he said. He retraced his steps to the kitchen and ordered Elsie's daughter to make him a large thermos of coffee. Then he turned to Kim. "You must stay here."

Kim returned to the bedroom and quickly tossed her things into her knapsack. There was no doubt in Kim's mind what she had to do. She moved so quickly that she almost ran head first into Elsie who had come to collect the untouched tea tray. When she saw the packed knapsack, Elsie held her hand over her mouth and cried out.

"No, no, child, you cannot go!" she said. "I will tell Madam."

"I'm not going anywhere," Kim lied. Then to distract Elsie she picked up the teapot and poured tea into the empty white cup. "This is for you," said Kim.

"No, no," Elsie said with alarm. "Miss Kim, I don't want any." Elsie glared again at Kim's knapsack.

Kim remembered something odd that had happened that morning. Riana had made coffee for Elsie in a china cup. Yet while Riana was out of the room Kim saw Elsie pour the coffee into the enamel mug that she kept for herself on a hook near the kitchen sink. "Old habits die hard," Riana had explained when Kim had asked about it. "In our household, like in many traditional ones, Africans did not drink and eat with the same utensils as us."

"Us?" Kim had asked.

"Whites." Riana had said.

"My mom is — near — the — fire," Kim said in a loud and staccato voice, as if Elsie was deaf. "I *have* to go!" But Elsie was no longer alone. Tante Reza was standing in front of her, her arms crossed over her chest.

"Where do you think you are going?" thundered her aunt.

"Nowhere," Kim said glaring down at the skirt of her aunt's black dress. The handgun was still peeking out of the pocket.

"I am locking this door until Marjike gets back to keep an eye on you," Tante Reza said. Then she pushed Elsie out and shut the door. Kim heard a sharp click.

How dare they lock her in! The need to escape was overwhelming. Kim flung open the window and saw that there was a tree close enough to climb down. Without thinking, she yanked on her jacket, tugged her knapsack on her back, and straddled the tree. In a few seconds she had jumped to the ground, scraping one of her hands in the process. She slipped into the back of Piet's 4 X 4 and hid under a tarp that was spread out in the back. No one came after her.

Just in time. A moment later Kim heard her uncle climb into the 4 X 4 and turn on the ignition. Soon the tires crunched on the gravel road and a remote control closed the gate behind them. Kim could hear the outside dogs barking as they ran loose behind the electric fence. They would patrol the area around the farmhouse until her uncle returned.

Once they passed the main farm gate, the road was much smoother. Kim heard her uncle roll down his window and flick his lighter. She smelled the cigarette almost at once. Twenty minutes passed, maybe more. The tarp was a tent over her head and eventually Kim found a safe way to peek through the back window.

In a matter of seconds they wound through her mom's old hometown, wet and shiny from the earlier rainstorm. "A shop, a bottle store, and a church," her mother had described it when they had arrived here by train five days ago. On the outskirts was the *onderdorp*, or lower town. Kim remembered how her mother had pointed it out to her. In the past everyone who was not white had to live in the onderdorp, and Riana had complained that it looked exactly the same as it always had. Rundown, lime-washed cottages with cement floors, no electricity, and no indoor plumbing, housed countless barefoot kids and their parents. "Condemned by the health officials," Riana had said with a sigh. At the time Riana's words meant nothing to Kim. Now she thought with a chill of Themba's words on the phone: "*You would not have been able to live where your mother lived. Or go to a white hospital. Your whole life would have been controlled. Controlled by them.*"

Kim lifted the tarp up an inch. Her last image of the lower town was a donkey cart rattling by, wet mud splattering under its wheels. She felt sick to imagine living here – forced by the government to exist in a slum because of the color of her skin.

As her uncle's Land Rover slipped back into the darkness past the town, weariness and numbness eventually melted through Kim's bones and calmed her. She thought of her mother and began to have a new sympathy for her. Now she understood why Riana was so determined to leave for Canada. What Kim did not understand is why her mother had kept so many secrets. Soon they would be in Lion's River and she would be able to ask her.

Kim had no idea how long she slept. She was wakened by the loud crackle of static on the radio unit in her uncle's car. Was there some news of the fire? It sounded like her aunt's voice shrieking in Afrikaans into the microphone. Uncle Piet answered in a few quiet words and finished with an "over and out." There was silence.

After a moment Oom Piet spoke. "Come and sit in the front, my girl. They took half an hour to discover you were missing."

Kim climbed out of her hiding place. She hoped her uncle was not going to be too mad at her. "I had to see my mother," she said, by way of explanation.

"Fine," Oom Piet fired back. He waved his cigarette at her. "I must smoke in my own car. I hope you have no problems with that."

"That's fine with me," said Kim as she scrambled into the passenger's seat and clicked on her seat belt. She started when she noticed the rifle on the floor of the Land Rover. "Is my mom okay?" she asked.

"I'm sure she is," answered her uncle. "I will leave you in town with her and go on to where they need help controlling the fire."

"When will we get there?" Kim asked.

"Twenty minutes or so."

There was still a bit of light left in the distance on the very tops of the purple-blue mountains. Her mother's Karoo spread out for miles around them. It swallowed them up with its vastness. It was still a desert even after a rainstorm.

"Did your ma tell you our town now has a colored mayor?" Oom Piet said after awhile. "The new flag flies in front of the police station. I was telling Riana that things have changed now and she can come home."

*Home is Canada*, Kim thought. But she was numb and tired and not up to any more arguments tonight. Oom Piet had already done enough for her by not being furious and taking her straight back to the farm.

He blew smoke out the open window and spoke. "While we were growing up, Riana's vision of a melting pot made no sense to me, or to our family. But history has proved us wrong."

Kim began to tap her foot against the side of the car. On the roadside, two black women walked one behind the other. They balanced shopping bags on their heads and had a long walk ahead of them. *Could this have been my life?* she wondered.

Oom Piet smoked and kept his eyes on the road. "I thought about going overseas. Your ma's flight had me thinking: Man, maybe I should take my family and leave, too."

Small winged creatures, larger than any insect Kim knew, plunged headfirst into the windshield. "Why didn't you go?" Kim asked.

After a moment her uncle turned to her. "I knew that to leave South Africa would be death for me. I can't leave. This is my home."

"It couldn't have been easy for Riana to leave either," Kim said in a rigid voice. "She loves this country too, you know. She would have stayed here forever if she could have. I mean if I hadn't happened."

"She would have left anyway, I think," Oom Piet said. "She was very unhappy with our country."

Kim's shoulders were tense and she had trouble swallowing. "A kid didn't make her escape any easier."

Oom Piet nodded solemnly.

Kim turned to him. "I know about my father. Why didn't she marry Hendrik? Was it because Oupa forbade it?"

Oom Piet crushed out his cigarette. "Oupa forbade it, yes. But the law at the time also forbade it."

"Why?" Kim asked.

Oom Piet stared at the road. "There was to be no mixing between Whites and Non-whites. That was the law. But your ma was in love with Hendrik."

Her mother had broken the law to have a relationship with the man she loved. Suddenly Kim was alert. The numbness she had felt earlier disappeared.

"Is that why Oupa burned down the compound and Lettie's house?" Kim asked. "Because my mom had broken the law?"

Her uncle pulled out a packet of gum. After Kim refused, he unwrapped a piece for himself. "Your grandfather was not thinking when he did that," he said as he bit down on the gum. "He was out of his mind with anger and fear. He had just lost Ouma, his wife, and he was blinded by his fear that he would lose his only daughter too." Oom Piet paused, chewed, and thought through his words. "Oupa could not harm his own daughter so he took it out on Lettie. He blamed Lettie for helping Riana and Hendrik. When everyone was away at church he set Lettie's room and all her belongings on fire. Then he banished her from the farm. Afterwards he was ashamed of what he had done, but was too proud to ask Lettie back. A few months later, with his approval, I bought the cottage in Cape Town and gave Lettie the job there. I agreed to pay for her children's school fees, anything, just to make it come right."

Kim angled the brooch that her grandfather had given her so it wouldn't dig into the flesh of her leg. She remembered how Themba had criticized Oom Piet for paying his school fees. Kim saw now that Oom Piet and her grandfather were trying to right their wrong. Without the money Themba would never have been able to go to a good school, have new uniforms, and expensive books.

"Why didn't Hendrik and my mom leave together for Canada?" Kim asked. "Why didn't they get married in Canada?"

Oom Piet shrugged. "That is a good question. Sorry. I don't know the answer. That was between your ma and Hendrik."

They drove without speaking. They could smell the fire now and Kim worried about her mother's safety.

"Why did the townspeople set the fires?"

"A few extremists did this. They don't trust the Truth Hearings," said her uncle. "They think it stirs up hatred for us, for the Afrikaners."

Kim glanced across at him. He frowned as he stared at the road.

"Luckily, the rains have begun," her uncle continued. "We have lived through many droughts. We know how the rain makes the land, the animals, and the people rejoice. Tomorrow you will see how the Karoo will have sprung to life. It will be a magnificent green. The rain, if it falls as far north as the town, might lessen the fire, too. Your mom will be safe," he added. "I promise you."

The light was almost gone. For the first time Kim felt close to her uncle. She was grateful that he was taking her to her mom and that he had answered so many of her questions, even though he could not answer the key ones about her father.

Oom Piet was searching for news but couldn't get a station to tune in properly. One channel played a jingle in Xhosa and Kim remembered all the times she had gone to Lettie's room and how Lettie always found a way to make her feel better. How could Lettie be so kind to Kim and Riana, after all the pain that Oupa had inflicted on her?

The radio station vanished into silence. Oom Piet flicked on his headlights as it had gotten quite dark. "Kim," he said. "Riana paid her price in leaving and we paid our price by staying. It is my hope that when you return to Canada, you remember where you come from."

Kim adjusted her great-grandmother's brooch deeper into her pocket.

"What do you see when you close your eyes?" he asked in a strange voice. He lit another cigarette and added, "I asked your mother that question the other day. She told me that when she closes her eyes she sees your yard in Canada all dressed up in snow.

How about that? What do I see when my eyes are shut? Our little baby girl Katie – gone."

Kim lifted her turtleneck up to her nose and smelled the fear from the wild ride on Willem trapped in the cloth. "What happened to Katie?" she whispered.

Uncle Piet's fingers that held the cigarette trembled. "It was during the time when there was a lot of unrest in the country. Many people were unhappy with apartheid. Your Tannie Reza was driving Elsie into the township when the car was stoned by black youths. Little Katie was strapped into the backseat of the car. She was hit in the head by a stone the size of a brick. My daughter did not suffer. She died instantly."

Kim's stomach squeezed tight and she could not speak. She thought of how Tante Reza always wore black and moved through the house like a ghost. How mean she had been to deride her aunt for her strange behavior.

A sudden blast of static from the radio unit interrupted Kim's thoughts. "*Piet, kom in! Piet, kom in!*" Piet grabbed the handset and adjusted a knob. "Piet here!" The line crackled and a male voice spoke in Afrikaans.

Kim let her turtleneck slip back into place. "What is happening?" she asked.

"It is good news," her uncle said pulling hard on the steeling wheel. "The wind has changed and the town is no longer being threatened."

A truck rumbled by. It was open in the back and filled with black and white men. "Look," said her uncle. "Those are volunteers. They will hack a firebreak with axes and spades." Her uncle pointed. "Look there, on the mountain."

They had come around a bend in the road and could finally see where the fire was. Red molten patches crisscrossed the mountainside. The mountain resembled an outraged volcano pouring out its lava.

For a few seconds Kim watched the fire spread its ruby-red destruction. "When will we get there?" she asked.

"Soon," said her uncle as he pressed his foot down on the gas pedal.

# SIXTEEN

# LION'S RIVER

"What are you doing here?" Riana cried as they rushed onto the veranda of the Lion's River Hotel. Behind Riana, brilliant pink and magenta flowers bloomed on the wall.

"I came to help with the fire," Piet explained.

Riana looked in outrage from Kim to her brother. "You shouldn't have brought Kim."

"Mom," Kim pleaded. "Don't blame him. I hid in the back without his knowing. I was worried about you."

"It's not a problem," said Piet.

Riana pushed her larger-than-life glasses up on her nose. "Don't make light of it," she snapped. "Don't do that to me, okay?"

Kim tried to keep her voice normal. "Please. Riana. You're always fighting with each other."

"We are not," insisted her mother, through clenched teeth.

"I heard you," said Kim. "Last week. You were screaming at Oom Piet and you were screaming at Oupa. You had my stuff spread out all over the table."

"Well, I needed photos!" Riana exclaimed. "Remember that first flat we lived in?"

"No, I don't." Kim reminded her. "I was only six months old!"

Oom Piet stepped forward, put his arm around Riana, and tried to calm her. Riana looked like she would wiggle away, but then Kim saw the space between them grow smaller and smaller. Riana blinked her doe eyes and allowed her brother to hug her. "You don't think I knew?" he said to her quietly. Then he turned to Kim, "Your ma needed to show us those photos so I would understood how very brave you both are," he said.

Kim looked at her feet. She was embarrassed to watch this rare exchange of affection.

"Well, maybe it's better that you're both here," Riana said as she pulled away. "I guess it really is. This has become a much bigger story than we first thought. I won't have time to return to the farm."

Piet met her eyes. "Riana, are you sure?"

"Pa and I talked. We did. I think he began to understand."

"All right. Then I'll say your good-byes for you when I get back."

Riana smiled at her brother. "*Ag, boetie*, thank you."

"Always my pleasure," he said. Then he hugged

Kim close to him. "Don't forget about us when you return to Canada. My girl, you are always welcome on the Milky Way Farm."

"Wait," said Kim as her uncle walked down the stairs of the veranda. Her throat was tight and suddenly, she didn't want him to leave. "I thought the fire was under control."

"Well, they still need help with it." He walked to his vehicle. "Bye-bye, hey," he said as he climbed inside and slammed the door.

*I won't cry, I won't cry*, Kim told herself. But right there on the hotel veranda, her eyes were blurred with tears. Her uncle was the first relative she had ever met. She did not know when she would see him again.

She cleared her throat and shouted, "Be careful, Oom Piet." But he had already started the Land Rover and did not near her. Cigarette between his teeth, he waved good-bye.

Kim rubbed her face on her shirt and watched her uncle disappear down the main street. Riana slipped her arm around Kim and they strolled past a white church with a spire and continued walking until they reached the outskirts of the town. It was dark and the stars were beginning to show in the sky. After a moment Kim spoke. "Oom Piet told me about Hendrik." There was a pause. "And he told me about Katie," Kim added.

Riana found Kim a tissue. "I was going to tell you about Katie when I thought you were old enough. Piet wrote to me about the funeral. Oupa bought a few boards of pine and built the small coffin himself. Afterwards Oupa retreated to his ark, pulled up the tall ladder, and would not come out for days."

Kim ignored the tissue and brought her sleeve up to her cheek. "Why didn't you go to the funeral?"

"You were only a month older than Katie at the time. I couldn't afford the air ticket. Besides, it was not a good time for them to see me."

*Not a good time for them to see me either*, thought Kim, shoving the unused tissue into her pocket. She felt the brooch that her grandfather had given her and took it out.

"Why would Oupa want me to have this?" she asked as she showed the heavy silver ornament to her mother. "Is it because he feels guilty about the past?"

Riana drew in her breath as she studied the brooch. "This was Great-Ouma's and was passed down to my mother. Oupa is getting old. I imagine he wanted to make amends before it's too late."

Suddenly in the darkness there was a drawn-out wail ending in a bark. "What was that?" Kim asked. She slipped the brooch in her pocket and moved closer to her mother.

"Just a jackal."

Kim shivered and looked up at the sky. There were more stars than Kim had ever seen, but there was no Big Dipper, no Little Dipper, and no constellation that Kim recognized. For a moment they stood saying nothing.

"Mom, are you going to be okay?"

"Yes. Yes I am. And I'm glad we decided not to stay an extra three months."

"And Andries?"

"Oh, that was nothing," Riana said quickly. "I'll be finished with this story tomorrow and we can leave the next day."

"Back to Cape Town?" asked Kim.

Riana nodded. "Yes. The amnesty hearing involving Themba's father is scheduled for Friday."

The air was cool as they walked back on the tree-lined road to the hotel. The croaking of crickets filled the night with shrill obsessive sounds like the questions in her head: *Who was her father? Why keep him a secret? Why did he not contact them?* Kim was about to ask but before she could, Riana's cell rang. It was her producer. He wanted a background story on one of the victims. Kim sighed as her mom promised to stay up late and finish off another report. Tonight would not be the time to get the answers Kim needed.

With Riana at work early the next morning, Kim explored Lion's River's main store. She had never seen a shop like this: it smelled of mothballs and talcum powder, and had everything in it from jawbreakers and half loaves of bread to clothes and household wares. As she stared at the long strips of yellow flypaper spiraling down from the ceiling, she tried to focus on the Afrikaans conversation between the ancient old clerk and a girl about her age in a school uniform. Kim was surprised by how much of the conversation she understood and was relieved to have some place to distract her thoughts. All morning she'd rehearsed various conversations she wanted to have with her mother. But she found her mind jumping to Hendrik. She had a lot to ask him as well. She imagined herself, calm as a detective, peppering him with questions, making him do the talking. In another scenario, her mind filled with accusations. *You must be hiding something! You didn't contact me. Not one lousy time.*

By late afternoon Kim had made her way to the hall where the hearings were taking place and waited outside for her mom. It was a warm afternoon and some of the journalists and lawyers were sipping cold drinks on small chairs and tables set out on polished red tiles. Kim sat away from them and dangled her long legs over the stoep wall. Riana had appeared briefly, dressed in hemp pants and a man's wrinkled white shirt.

"Mom," Kim had pleaded. "At least tuck in your shirt." Reluctantly Riana did as she was told before she darted inside to say good-bye to colleagues. Now Kim sat with a messy pile of Riana's belongings: her battered leather bag, sweater, tape recorder, glasses, and notes.

Kim enjoyed the sensation of letting her eyelids close and open in the cozy heat of the stoep. The sun was dropping in the sky, tinting everything lime-green and gold. The vegetation had changed, sprung to life, just as Oom Piet had promised.

She could hear distant cheers from a cricket game as it wound down. Occasionally, a car went by on the dusty road in front of the hall. It would soon be evening. Kim remembered the girl in the shop, and wondered how she passed her time in a small town like this. Bored, Kim set her mom's tape recorder on her lap and pushed the PLAY button.

A hoarse female voice with a heavy African accent spoke. "When I went to the police to ask about my parents they said I must go to the mortuary. An uncle took me and we identified the bodies. 'Are you sure?' they asked us. 'Yes,' we answered. 'We are sure.' From that moment my life changed forever. I was fourteen at the time and I had to be mother and father to the younger children. I could not finish school. I could not take a job outside the house. I could not take opportunities. You see, sir, my parents' death was a murder. But our family unit was murdered too."

A hawker with bags of tomatoes in his arms strolled past the veranda, chanting: "Five rands a bunch. Five rands a bunch." Kim turned her attention back to the tape. The next speaker was a man with a deep distinct voice. "I dreamed of studying abroad," he began. "Ja, I had dreams like that. 'Solly Bosman, you are a born professor,' the aunties told me often. But I did not further my education. My problems began when I got a job teaching school, but I did not teach the curriculum that was expected. Instead, I taught the real history using the names of our legitimate heroes and leaders. The principal took me aside and asked: 'Why, Solly? Why be an agitator? It is dangerous because the white authorities are watching you.' It was not the end of the story. One day the police came into my class-room and took me away. Not to the station but to a deserted farm. They hung me upside down. They put electric shocks on the bottoms of my feet and later dropped me off the roof of the barn. They wanted me to denounce my students, give up the names of those who had participated in rallies. When I would not, they shocked me again. This time in my inti-mate parts." He cleared his throat and added, "Even today, Mr. Chairman, because of these injuries, my manhood is diminished. And I have no longer use of my legs because of the fall from the barn roof."

Kim clicked the STOP button. In the field across from her, a school group was packing up a picnic. Straw hats bobbed up and down with laughter. She trembled as she put her mom's tape recorder back in the leather bag.

"Solly, would you like a cool drink?" boomed a voice behind her. Kim turned to see a tall, brown-skinned man enter the stoep beside a man in a wheelchair. They had just come out of the hearings and they were both dressed in suits.

"I'm fine," said the man in the wheelchair. "But I'm glad that is behind me. Thanks, man, for bringing me up here."

Kim froze. She recognized the male voice. It was the one on her mom's tape.

The man wheeled himself close to where Kim sat. She couldn't help but stare at him. "Afternoon," he said to her. He had short gray hair and thick glasses.

"Hello," said Kim, suddenly shy. A car squealed to a stop in front of them, and Kim was relieved to have this distraction. Everyone on the stoep turned to stare. The driver got out, and squatted down to look underneath the car. A skinny woman with blonde cascading hair flung open the passenger door. "It was a rock!" she cried in an American accent. "It was a rock the size of a tortoise."

"Sure enough," grumbled the driver. "Water is dripping onto the ground."

The man in the wheelchair turned to Kim. "Look, the foreign journalists are having troubles with their rented car."

The tall man went forward. "The petrol station is closed for the night. How far must you travel?" he asked the American couple.

The man looked up at him. "Only a few miles. We are staying at Bushbaby Camp."

The tall man called to a waitress. "Mama, please bring me some Sunlight soap," he said.

"Come, Hendrik, what are you up to now?" laughed the man in the wheelchair.

In a moment the waitress came back with a bar of soap.

"I will take chips off the soap and massage them between my palms," he explained. Kim watched as he scraped slivers of soap off with his thumbnail. Then he kneaded them between his hands. "Look what I get – 'Plasticine.'"

The tall man pushed the putty into the crack in the radiator. "In the morning ask someone at the petrol station to fix the leak," he said as he straightened up.

"Thanks a million," said the American journalist. "Can we give you a ride?"

"No, thank you," he responded. "We are traveling all the way back to Cape Town tonight and we have our own car."

The Americans drove off. The terrace was growing dark. The waitress brought out candles and set them on the tables. Then the man in the wheelchair spoke to Kim. "Do you know the time?"

Kim looked at her watch. "Six o'clock," she said.

The tall man stooped forward to look at Kim. "I detect an accent," he said with a smile.

"I'm Canadian," said Kim. "My mom's a journalist."

Kim stared right into his eyes. They were gentle, wrinkled up with his smile. "A Canadian journalist?" he asked.

"My mom's South African. She grew up on a farm near here. But we live in Canada now."

The handicapped man pivoted his chair around. "I will use the nice toilets here before we go. Just think, Hendrik, the cubicles have been constructed not only for Africans, but for Africans in wheelchairs," he added with a laugh as he wheeled himself into the building.

Kim and the tall man were alone. Kim wondered why he was staring at her.

"Have you been in South Africa long?" he asked.

"Almost three months."

"Well, what do you think of our country?"

Kim wasn't sure what she was going to say until she spoke. "I'm glad my mom brought me."

They both looked past the twisted aloes and thorn trees to the empty Karoo veld beyond the town. The land that spread out in front of them looked raw and prehistoric in the dimness.

At that moment Riana returned. Her white shirt was only half tucked in at the waist and she had a paper cup of coffee. She stopped dead when she saw the face of the man standing beside Kim.

Riana put her coffee down on a table. She was very pale.

"My God," said the tall man. "Riana. Let me look at you."

Kim swallowed. Her heart was beating into her ears. Riana stepped back.

The man cleared his throat and turned to Kim: "My name is Hendrik Fortune. I'm your father."

# SEVENTEEN

# "THEMBA FOUND HIM"

The next morning Riana got up early to pack for the long ride to Cape Town. While her mother was in the bathroom, Kim lay fully dressed on her hotel bed listening to bird noises and reliving the unexpected meeting with her father. Today she could hardly remember what he looked like. He was tall with brown skin — more than a tan, she thought — and gentle eyes. He had laughed when Kim told Riana how he'd put soap putty on the radiator of the Americans' car. Hendrik and Riana hardly spoke. They kept looking at each other like they were seeing ghosts. But before Hendrik left, he had asked if they could meet in Cape Town. He gave them his card. Soon after, he wished them a safe journey and left with his friend.

Riana interrupted Kim's thoughts by plopping a container and plastic spoon into her hands.

"What's this?" Kim asked.

"Pot-pudding," Riana said. "One of the translators gave it to me." Kim tasted it and declared it delicious. "We'll take the rest with us," said her mother. "We need to get on the road. Come on. It's going to rain."

Blue-black clouds were forming when they climbed into the rental car. Riana sipped a coffee and stared at the road ahead of them. Kim was concerned about her. Since they had seen Hendrik, Riana had withdrawn into her own world.

"Are you upset about yesterday?"

Riana shifted gears. The bottom of the rental car scraped the dirt road. "No, I'm fine."

Kim settled into her seat and watched the bush spread for miles in front of the low hills beyond.

"What should I call him?" Kim asked after some time had passed. They were still on a dirt road, had to go slow, and then finally stop altogether to allow a few cows to cross the road. "Hendrik? Mr. Fortune? Dad?"

Riana drummed her hand on the steering wheel. The cattle passed and the rental car rattled and gained speed. Rain in the night had made the land less thirsty and given life to the bush. Still, the dust was everywhere, and they had to shut the windows tight to keep it out of the car.

Kim opened the container of pot-pudding and shared with Riana. Riana wiped some off the corner of her mouth. "Themba's grandmother, Elsie, used to make this on the farm," she said. "Elsie was like a mother to me. When I was little she put me on her back in a sling and carried me all over the farm. When I was older she washed my grazed knees and rocked me when I was sick. Then, one day, I realized that she had her own children." Riana paused. Her mouth stiffened. "It was quite a shock. It had never occurred to me until she showed me the photos of Lettie and Rosie. They were with relatives in the Transkei. By law they were not allowed to live with her. I never realized that by raising me, providing me with all the comfort and beauty that she did, she was missing her own children."

Kim stared at her mom. It was as if the pudding had loosened a rush of memories.

Riana swirled her plastic spoon through the thick pudding and continued. "When I was your age, I went to school, sitting on the leather seats of my parent's car, my ankles crossed neatly in little white socks. I was happy with my life. I trusted it. I didn't ask questions. I didn't think to ask why it was that only Blacks formed lines in the sun at bus stops. My mind was always on some bit of homework, pleasing a teacher, getting a good grade."

The pot-pudding was finished. Kim took a gulp of water from her bottle. A car passed them and streaked off down the road, a brown cloud rising behind it. The sky had grown dark. Large, noisy raindrops spattered down.

Riana continued, "I was a naive farm girl. But by the time I enrolled at university, I was beginning to wake up, albeit slowly. I was nineteen and this part has to do with your father. We were both at the University of Cape Town, a multiracial institution. It had been a huge fight for me to attend. Oupa and Ouma were dead set against it, but in the end I won – only because I told them I wouldn't go at all if I couldn't go there. It was the first time I met people of different backgrounds as equals, as friends. For almost fifty years apartheid forced the people of South Africa to live apart as Blacks, Whites, Indians, and Coloreds. I never really knew until then what the laws meant. How everything my life was based on – all the beauty and safety – was a lie! And it was Hendrik who showed me the lies."

"How did he do that?" Kim was anxious to keep her mom talking.

Riana kept her eyes on the road. The rain was so heavy she was having trouble seeing. The windows were fogging up. She wound her window down a crack and then reached across and opened Kim's.

Kim watched a few drops bounce on her arm. "You were talking about Hendrik," she reminded her mom.

Riana nodded. "He showed me things about the country that I was blind to," she continued. "Hendrik had the kindest way of doing that. He never blamed me personally, always the system. He said we were all victims of apartheid, no matter what color our skin. I fell in love with his kindness. But at first I would not admit it to myself. He was so frighteningly different from me. I judged him as my parents would."

"What changed your mind?" asked Kim.

"One day on campus we tried to protest the racist laws. We were tear gassed. Because it was a predominately white university we were only shot at with rubber bullets, but some were arrested. Hendrik was one of the few who was. They chose him because he was not white, and they detained him for a couple of weeks. I was frantic. He came back to me with three cracked ribs, a split eyebrow, broken teeth. I nursed him and fell in love with him."

Kim tried to memorize every detail that Riana gave her. "Why didn't you ever tell me about Hendrik?" she asked. "I mean that he wasn't white. Why leave out that little fact? Did you think I would care? Were you ashamed of him?"

"I loved him." Riana said quickly. "I really did."

"And you never felt embarrassed by the color of his skin?"

"No," Riana said looking Kim in the eye. "I just wanted to leave all that behind. I didn't want to think it mattered."

"But it does matter!" cried Kim. "I can't run away from it like you. And I don't want to. It's part of me. Part of who I am."

For a moment they drove in silence. They came to a small town, slowing down as they passed a church and corner shop. At one end of the town it was raining. The other end was dry. The car passed through the town in a few seconds.

"Why didn't Hendrik go with you to Canada?" Kim asked.

"I wanted him to come," Riana said. "I begged him to come!"

"He said no?"

Riana turned the car onto the highway, changed gears, and accelerated. "Hendrik was very politically involved. People in his organization advised him against it."

"And he listened to them?"

"Yes," Riana said. "When I became pregnant I gave him an ultimatum. I told him that I couldn't be married to the struggle. I couldn't be married to the movement. I needed him to come with me, or that would be it. His child would have no father."

Riana slipped her sunglasses over her eyes and continued. "When I first arrived in Canada, I wanted to call him. So many times I wanted to. But I needed a clean break. It was the only way I could stay strong and leave my country. Eventually we fell out of contact." Riana took a deep intake of air. "It was Themba who tracked him down."

Kim was astonished by this piece of news. "Themba found him?"

Riana nodded yes. "The other morning Themba called me on my cell. He couldn't reach you at the farm. Last week in a bookstore in Cape Town, Themba found a book that Hendrik had written. He left a message for him at his South African publisher's office. When Hendrik rang, Themba told him I was covering the hearing at Lion's River."

"Why didn't Themba mention this when I spoke to him?" Kim asked.

"He wanted to wait until he made contact. He didn't want to get your hopes up."

Kim thought about the day she had phoned Themba from the farm. It must have been hard for him not to share his discovery with her. He didn't tell her that he had found Hendrik's book because he was protecting her from disappointment. She had never had such a loyal friend.

"I am glad you have decided to meet with him again," Riana added after a moment. "For the real questions that you have, Hendrik is the only one who can give you the answers."

Kim sat beside her mother in silence. She couldn't tell if they had driven for one hour or four. Her head was spinning. Every piece of information led to a new question. Maybe it was Hendrik who was ashamed! Maybe he was ashamed of his daughter.

Kim asked, "I wonder why he never wrote to me — never sent me a single letter?"

Keeping her eyes on the road, her mother answered. "You'll have to ask him that."

# EIGHTEEN

# THE AMNESTY HEARING

The parking lot outside the building where the Cape Town Truth and Reconciliation Commission Hearings would be held was filling up fast. At the same moment that Riana spied an empty parking place, Kim noticed Themba standing on the entranceway steps. "Let me out," she said. "I want to talk to Themba while you park."

Kim got out of the car and crossed quickly to where Themba was.

"So, I made it," Themba said in his half mocking voice. His dark eyes met hers. "Good to see you."

Kim nodded. It was wonderful to see him again. But today was not going to be easy. They had spoken the night before on the phone and, even though he was still threatening not to attend the hearing, Kim suspected that deep in his heart Themba wanted to go.

Kim shielded her eyes from the bright sun. "Where is everyone?" she asked. She knew that Grandfather Khanyisa, Ntombi, and Sophie had all planned to be there.

"Inside," he said.

Kim studied his face and saw that he was trembling.

"What would you do?" he asked her.

"I don't know," said Kim. "I guess I'd go in. To back up my mom."

Themba's response was barely audible. "I will see him," he said. "I will see my father's killer. And then he will walk free."

Kim almost touched Themba's shoulder but before she could do so, her mom joined them.

"Hello, Themba," Riana said. "Let's hurry and go inside. These hearings have a reputation for starting on time."

Riana ushered them up the stairs to the entrance. As they entered the building, Themba followed. *Maybe he's been waiting for me to arrive*, Kim thought. *Or maybe he just needed a gentle push to go in.*

"Do you want to sit with us?" Kim asked as they came to the large room where the hearing would take place. Themba shook his head and whispered that he would sit with his family.

Kim waved as he crossed the room. She watched him slip into a seat with his grandfather on one side, and Ntombi, and his sister, Sophie, on the other. Kim hardly recognized Ntombi: she was dressed formally and her brown face was expressionless. Grandfather Khanyisa kept swallowing and touching his Adam's apple as if something was stuck in his throat.

Riana and Kim took their seats beside Andries. Kim didn't want to sit with Andries, but they needed to be on the aisle and in the section reserved for the media. Earlier Kim had promised her mother that she would leave immediately if Riana told her to. It was the only way she would allow Kim to attend the hearing. Her mother did not want Kim to hear any grisly details of the murder.

The hearing was getting underway. The judge and the commissioners sat behind a long table, elevated slightly above the participants. Nearby sat the translators, provided for people who wanted to speak in their mother language and not English. There were two smaller tables, one on each side of the room.

Lettie sat at one of the small tables, dressed in a dark suit and beret. She took her glasses out of their case, set them on the table in front of her, and folded her hands in her lap, staring ahead silently while the lawyer beside her busied himself with some papers. At the opposite table sat another lawyer and a stocky white man in khaki trousers, shirt, and tie. Kim watched him shift his heavy body in the chair and whispered to her mother. Riana confirmed it. This was the former policeman who had abducted Themba's father from his house seven years ago.

The head commissioner rose, welcomed everyone, and began with a few sentences to set the tone for the amnesty hearing. "Mr. Chairperson," he said, adjusting his microphone, "I want to thank all the people who have come forward in the name of truth to stand before this hearing today."

Kim turned her attention away from the head commissioner and studied the man dressed in khaki. *This is what a killer looks like*, Kim thought. She had expected this man to have a thick, bull face and evil expression. Instead, the former policeman had a neat mustache, freshly cut hair, and pale skin. Kim was astonished to see that he looked ordinary.

The commissioner was finishing off his opening remarks. "What we hope to demonstrate by these hearings is the African principle of *ubuntu*, which means 'reconciliation.' The primary goal of these hearings is to lay bare the roots of apartheid so that this can never happen again. In the words of the Archbishop Desmond Tutu: 'Without forgiveness there is no future, but without confession there can be no forgiveness.'"

Kim glanced across the room at Themba. He remained motionless.

The commissioner sat down as people shifted in their seats. The lawyer who was representing the ex-policeman stood and told the court his client's name. "Gert van Niekerk is seeking amnesty," he began. "It is to do with his part in the assault and death of Mr. Sandile Bandla."

"Mr. van Niekerk," said one of the judges. "Please stand and raise your right hand. Do you swear to tell the truth, the whole truth and nothing but the truth so help you God?"

"I do," said the ex-policeman. He sat down and folded his hands one into the other.

"Proceed," said the head commissioner.

"The date in question was March 30, 1990," the lawyer began. "What, in your words, were the circumstances behind entering Mr. Sandile Bandla's house early in the morning of that day?"

The ex-policeman leaned his forearms on the table and spoke slowly into his microphone. "We were told that Sandile Bandla lived in that house. He was understood to be a leader in boycotts and anti-apartheid incidents. I was carrying out orders." He looked at the lawyer and not at Lettie or her family. A muscle twitched in the side of his face. Beside Kim, Riana and Andries scribbled furiously in their notebooks.

A man in a navy suit, the lawyer who represented the commission, got to his feet to ask a question. "You were defending apartheid?"

The ex-policeman nodded. "It was my job to do so."

"How many people did you assault per week?"

The ex-policeman took a quick sip of water. "About three or four."

"How many of those whom you assaulted died each week?"

The ex-policeman's lawyer intervened. "Mr. Chairman, could we keep the questioning to the incident at hand?" he asked.

Again, Kim looked over at Themba; he sat stiff in his chair, his eyes boring into the face of the policeman. Beside Themba, Ntombi could not keep still, and she kept passing her hand across her mouth.

"Tell us what happened on that night," the lawyer said.

"We entered the house by the front door," Van Niekerk continued in a thick accent, very much like Riana's. "I did not take into consideration that there might be small children in the house. We wanted Sandile Bandla, he was the target, but I saw at once that there were youngsters hiding under the bed." He paused, cleared his throat and continued. "I did not tell my superior officer, Captain van Rooi, about the children."

"Go on," said the lawyer.

Van Niekerk continued, "We found Sandile Bandla hiding in a shed-like structure attached to the side of the house."

"Did Mr. Bandla struggle?" asked the lawyer.

The ex-policeman paused, as if trying to get his bearings. "I believe so, yes," he mumbled. "Captain van Rooi instructed us to strike the terrorist with our sticks and fists."

Lettie shut her eyes as if praying.

"Sticks and fists?" repeated the lawyer, pulling his eyebrows together. "What happened then?"

The man did not answer. Riana pressed her notebook shut and put her arm on Kim's.

"I recall that Sandile Bandla fought back," Van Niekerk said. He paused, as if he was having trouble breathing, and then added: "I had to strike him quite a few times."

The lawyer raised his voice. "What happened then?" he asked.

"I managed to get one of his bare feet in my hands," the ex-policeman began and stopped. He blinked and added: "I pulled him into the back of the van. Then I tied a sack over his head."

Riana nudged Kim. Kim gave in and silently and they slipped out. In the corridor, Riana took a drink from a water fountain and then moistened her temples. Kim felt sick. "*One of his bare feet in my hands*" repeated itself over and over in her mind.

"Why?" she asked. "Why did he hate him so much?"

"He thought that Sandile was a terrorist," Riana explained. "He thought the Africans would take over the country, make it communist, and run it into the ground."

"Is that what Oupa and Oom Piet thought too?" Kim asked.

Riana paused and then looked off into space. "Yes," she answered.

One or two of the hall doors were open and inside Kim could see many safes and filing cabinets. She wondered if it was in these cabinets that all the secret confessions of the hearings were kept.

"Will that man really get off for murdering Sandile?" Kim asked. Her throat was very dry.

"He'll get amnesty – yes – I imagine," Riana said. Her body was stiff and her shoulders were up by her ears. "The applicant must make full disclosure of all the facts."

Kim was worried. Her mom was using her journalist voice, the voice she used when she did not want to feel something fully.

"Lettie will be able to have a proper burial," Riana continued in her I-will-feel-nothing radio voice. "The amnesty rules say that Van Niekerk must tell the hearing of Sandile's whereabouts."

"His body, you mean."

"Yes, his body," answered Riana quickly.

"This is a terrible way to make a living," Kim said. She was trying to joke – to ease the tension that was building in her mom's face, but it didn't work. In fact, Riana's face crumpled. She was in tears.

"I followed orders, too," said Riana softly crying. "Just like that policeman, I blindly moved from one safe pocket of white civilization to another – from the library to the shopping mall to the club. I didn't ask why Blacks went to different schools and hospitals. I didn't ask why I was served first in a line. I didn't ask why Elsie's children couldn't live with her. I trusted my country! Can you understand that? Like you trust Canada, I trusted South Africa! If I hadn't met your father, I might still have believed in it."

Kim found her mom a tissue. If she wasn't careful she would start to cry too. "Don't you need to get back?" she asked.

Riana composed herself and said: "Well, yes, I do."

Suddenly, Kim remembered something she had been wanting to ask ever since the fight at school. "What about my summer vacation? Our time here is short, and I hate that school. Since we're leaving anyway . . ."

Riana smiled. "Don't worry, you don't have to go anymore. I'll let them know you won't be returning."

Kim pointed to a nearby bench. Thanks. "I'll wait here for you."

Riana blew her nose and turned to Kim. "Darling, I'm sorry. I love you. You know that, don't you?"

Kim smiled shyly. "I know that," she said blinking back the tears.

After her mom was gone, Kim sat down. The corridor was quiet except for the odd person walking down the halls carrying files or coffees. Across from her on the wall was a poster. *The Truth Sets You Free*, it read.

At the end of the hall was a large, closed-circuit TV that was showing the hearing live. Suddenly Kim's eyes focused on the monitor. It was Lettie. Kim got to her feet and went closer so she could hear.

Lettie had asked to speak and a lawyer adjusted the microphone so it was closer to her mouth. She cleared her throat and began.

"Mr. Chairman, I am here today with my son, daughter, and young sister-in-law, the only remaining sibling of Sandile. I am also here with Sandile's father. He and I have witnessed this troubled country get to its feet, stumble, and go on, and we have voted recently for the first time in our lives. The decision, however, to attend this hearing was mine and mine alone. It may seem hard for some to understand why. I accepted that Sandile was dead, but I decided to come here today to learn the truth of his death and to ask this man who is responsible what happened to my husband's body." Lettie swallowed twice. "My heart is very heavy after hearing his confession, but some questions that have lived with me for the last seven years, have now been answered. Finally, my family will have a proper burial for my husband. I thank the chairman for hearing my case." She raised her chin. "God bless Africa."

There was a close-up of Van Niekerk who, after hearing Lettie's words, sat impassive. Then the camera focused on Lettie who refused a glass of water offered to her by the lawyer. The chairman called a short recess.

Kim turned away from the monitor and walked back to the water fountain. At first she didn't swallow anything, letting the cool water run through her mouth. Above her was another Truth and Reconciliation Commission poster with a cartoon figure on it. Directly on the heart, where the victim had been shot, was a gaudy red blob.

"Man, whose bright idea was this? To portray the victim like a cartoon character?"

She wheeled around. It was Themba. She had forgotten to tell him that her mother might make her leave the hearing halfway through.

"I'm sorry about what happened to your dad," Kim offered as she wiped water droplets from her chin.

Themba stood stiffly by her side. Kim didn't know what else to say.

Themba began to pace. His steps were heavy. It was as if his emotions were bound up in each step he took. "What was it like?" he said between clenched teeth. "To sit in the room and see with my own eyes the man who killed my father? Archbishop Tutu says it; President Mandela says it: *Nou kan ons gesels.* We have to talk to heal. Sweet words. But it doesn't bring Pa back."

Themba glared at the brightly colored poster, avoiding Kim's eyes. "You want to know why I pushed you so hard to find your pa? Even if this sounds stupid and childish, I was on an adventure. I was starring in a movie where lost daddies and missing fathers could be found." He squared his shoulders. "But today Gert van Niekerk's words changed all that. Themba Bandla must now act his age."

He took a small drink of water from the fountain. "I wish you had met him," he said. "He loved soccer and he taught me how to play it. People in the township talk about him still: how he played it very calmly, with great speed. As you know this is how it should be played." He paused. "Soccer was everything to him. A friend of his once told me that to him soccer was freedom." He smiled. "Promise you won't tell your ma that," he said. "I don't want to end up quoted on the radio."

"I promise."

"Thanks for being here. Come back with me. It is all over except the closing procedures. If you want, you can sit with us."

Kim inhaled sharply. Themba had invited her to sit on the side with him, Lettie, and their relatives. It was an honor to be included like that.

"Thanks," she said. "I'd love to sit with you."

Kim followed him back to the hearing room to where Sophie, Ntombi, and Grandpa Khanyisa sat waiting. She waved at her mom. The hearing was underway again and suddenly the people in the audience were singing.

"*Senzeni na, senzeni na . . .*"

"What does it mean?" Kim asked.

Themba's eyes were moist. "They are singing, '*What have we done? Our only sin is the color of our skin.*'"

# NINETEEN

# DISTRICT SIX

"Your mother claims you're my girl," Hendrik said as he parked the car. "Some people are easily taken in."

Kim stiffened when she heard his words, but relaxed when he winked at her. She flung open the car door and got out. It was a fine spring afternoon but Kim was too nervous to notice its beauty.

Hendrik was so tall that he stooped slightly as he walked beside her. "I have a photo of myself at your age," he said, as he directed her toward a dirt path. "It could be you – spitting image."

Why had she selected this shirt to wear today? To make matters worse, her hair had gone wild that morning and she was so nervous about meeting her father that she had forgotten to tie it back.

Kim and Hendrik were in the middle of a wide-open field. The wind was nonstop and it caused her ruffled blouse and her hair to flutter every which way.

"Right up there used to be the Seven Steps," Hendrik pointed as he scanned the horizon for landmarks. Kim liked his deep voice. "Charlie Jacobs, Apie Ismail, Solly Bosman," he said. "You remember Solly. You met him in Lion's River." Kim nodded. "We grew up together in District Six. We sat together on top of the Seven Steps, *slukking* down those big swollen bottles of Coke. Indian snake charmers, gangsters, poets – you name it – the Seven Steps were a hangout for all sorts. Ja, everyone who lived in the Six loved the Seven Steps. They too, were demolished like the rest of the place." He took out a chocolate bar and offered Kim some.

She was too nervous to eat. "Why was the district torn down?"

Hendrik put the chocolate away. "They didn't want the colored community living so close to the white areas, so they moved us all out and set the bulldozers to work. Everything came down but the churches and mosques. I'll never forget the day it happened. My pa was angry as hell and would not, under any circumstances, leave the house that his pa had built. They'd be looking for a black eye if they touched a brick of his house. True's God, we thought he'd be bulldozed right along with our home."

Kim's eyes followed where Hendrik was pointing but it was impossible for her to imagine where his boyhood house had stood. There was not a single fence or dwelling left anywhere. All that remained of the old district were the dome of a mosque and the steeple of a church.

"Where did your family move to?" Kim asked.

"My family was moved to the Flats, far out of Cape Town," Hendrik continued angrily, as he led her along the path. "Home was a small brick house with no trees. Sand and dust and wind always in our eyes. Our old neighbors were spread all around — never saw them again. Pa never adjusted to the move, the losses — finished him off, and he died soon afterwards."

Hendrik pointed toward the edge of the hill. "Just over there was the cinema. How about that? We called it the Bioscope in those days."

"Bioscope," Kim repeated the strange word.

"That's it," He nodded. He ran his fingers through his short, cropped hair and then stood very erect as he turned to look at her. "*Sê vir my*, do you know any Afrikaans at all?" He attempted a smile.

"*Buy-a-donkey*," Kim answered, smiling. But it was a fake smile. Her guard was up. She felt stiff inside; she had no way of knowing what was the proper way to act.

Hendrik was also on edge. He tried to laugh. "How am I doing?" he asked.

Kim looked up in surprise.

He said: "Impressions. Good or bad? It's not

easy, hey, to do this. I mean, I meet new people every day in my job, but – this, man – this is special."

Kim nodded. She was relieved that he had said what she was feeling. "I think you're doing fine," she told him.

He smiled. "You're more grown up than I thought."

*Is he crazy? Can't he see how my hands are shaking?* Kim thought. "When I found out you were in South Africa, my heart was bouncing out of my frame," he said. "I wanted to meet you so badly. So did Ginger." He looked at her with his almost black eyes. "Would you like to go somewhere to get some food?"

Kim shook her head. No way. She was feeling queasy enough. Eating was out of the question. "Who's Ginger?" she asked.

"Ginger's my girl. She's eight."

"Oh," said Kim. She was trying to figure out how Ginger would be related to her. It took her a moment to realize she would be a half sister.

Hendrik opened his bag and gave Kim something he had for her. "*Catcher in the Rye,*" he said as he handed it to her. "My favorite boyhood book."

"Thanks," Kim said. She wished she had something to give him but she hadn't thought of it. Instead, she said, "Mom told me you write books."

Hendrik smiled. "Lately I write invoices. I write memos. I'm struggling through a second book."

Kim set her small knapsack down on the path and pulled out the notebook. "Mom gave me this. I think it was yours."

He squatted down beside her.

"I wondered why you spelled Africa with a *K*?" she asked.

He studied the words that were scribbled there. "Some of us wanted to take the Colonial *C* out of the word *Africa* and make it a political word. Others used the *K* to make it a word derived from *Africa*. For your ma and me *Afrika* was the way we spelt the word since we were children, in our mother tongue."

Kim looked at him with surprise. "You and my mom have the same mother language?"

Hendrik nodded yes. "*Ons praat Afrikaans.*"

Kim would never understand all the complexities of this country.

Hendrik pointed at an entry in the notebook. "Look at the date: August, 1982. It was around the time I met your mother." He pulled the notebook closer. "This was written after a funeral. Can I translate it for you?"

Kim nodded and Hendrik began: "*Crowds, songs, flags, buffel tanks and Mello Yellows, stampeding people, coughing, blinded by tear gas.*"

He glanced up at her. "A guy I'd known since

primary school was shot in the face by police. At his funeral there was mayhem. People carried banners, not guns. The police attacked the funeral and three people lost their lives. At these three funerals there was more violence. More killing. I write here: '*How can this be all caused by a teenage boy who was shot going to the store for a loaf of bread?*'" He slowly straightened up.

Kim stood as well. "Do you want it back?" she asked. She did not really want to return the notebook to him.

His eyes met hers. "Kim, I want you to have it," he said. "We live in a different country now, but we should never be allowed to forget the past."

Relieved, Kim put the notebook back in her bag. Hendrik led her to the car and opened the door for her. "When do you and Riana leave for Canada?" he asked.

"In eight days."

"I am hoping I can see you again." He paused and added, "Ginger is very excited to meet you. And about having a half sister."

Kim climbed into the car. She was curious to meet Ginger but hadn't known how to suggest it. "I think that would be okay," she said.

His eyes lit up at her response. "Shall we go up Table Mountain and see the view?" he asked.

"Right now?"

"Ja. If you have time."

"Sure!" Kim said. She was relieved that he was not taking her home just yet. Time was running out and she had not asked him the important questions.

# TWENTY

# TABLE MOUNTAIN

They drove through the city in silence. Hendrik brought out the chocolate again. This time Kim took a piece. Driving with her father was so different from riding in the car with Oom Piet. Hendrik's hands were large and took up a lot of space on the steering wheel. They finished off the bar together.

"Do you play sports?" he asked, keeping his eyes on the road.

"I play soccer," Kim said. "Junior League."

"What position?" he asked.

"Forward. I missed a whole season to be here."

They turned up a steep road and parked near the cable car. "The wind's died down," he said. "Would you like to go up?"

"Yes!" Kim said. She knew her mom would never take her. It was midweek and the cable car was deserted. Hendrik purchased two tickets.

Kim steadied herself as the cable car twirled away from the platform and climbed high above the parking lot. They moved away from the ground quickly. Her stomach lifted and then dropped.

"Are you okay?" he asked.

"Butterflies in my stomach," she giggled. "It's wonderful."

"Your mom and I used to come up here."

"No way. Mom hates heights."

He smiled. "Ja, she does, but it was one of the few places we could go on dates. We hoped people would think we were tourists and leave us alone."

Kim tried to imagine her parents as young people. Hendrik had an open boyish face, yet he now had some gray, wiry, jack-in-the-box strands jumping out from his cropped hair. As for Riana, it was hard to imagine her as anyone other than her mom.

Thinking about her mother reminded Kim of all the questions she needed to ask. She was slightly more relaxed with Hendrik but he was still basically a stranger. He sensed her tension.

"What is it?" he asked.

"It's hard to imagine Mom going on dates," Kim answered.

Hendrik placed his large hands on the window of the cable car and stared down. "Your mom was so perfect. Around her I was afraid of making a fool of myself or setting a foot wrong. After class she gave up going out to restaurants and cocktail lounges to be with me. She wanted so much for me – as a writer, I mean." He paused briefly. "She believed in me. Without that belief I never would have finished my book."

*Mom*, Kim wanted to shout, *hid you from me!* But in front of the conductor Kim didn't say a word. Instead, she glared down at the harbor. Far into the bay she could see Robben Island.

When they finally arrived at the top, the conductor opened the door for his passengers. As soon as the cable car moved away, she turned to Hendrik. She blurted the words out quickly, before she changed her mind. "Mom, never once showed me your photo," she said in a shaky voice. "She kept you hidden from me!"

If Kim sounded rude, she didn't care. She was suddenly furious. It was as if this was only about Hendrik. If her words bothered him he didn't appear to be affected. He led Kim up the trail.

She couldn't look at him. "Like a convict!" she added sharply, just so he would get the point.

"I'm not surprised," he answered calmly.

"You're not *surprised!*" Kim repeated, stumbling on a rock. Hendrik helped her find her balance. She pulled her arm away from him. "You never contacted us!" Her voice broke. "You never once made an effort —"

Hendrik interrupted. "Kim, we had to keep it a secret. It was 1984, the height of apartheid. I was deeply involved in politics. Even after she left for Canada, we just had to keep that secret sealed up."

Kim struggled to understand why Hendrik and her mother needed to keep their relationship a secret, even when Riana was in another country.

Hendrik read her mind. "The truth is," he said, "I loved your mother, but I *was* selfish. The relationship would have harmed me."

The wind blew across Kim's face. "Because it was illegal?"

"Our relationship wasn't just illegal," he explained. "Your ma was white and an Afrikaner. In my organization some people were against mixing with Whites. Your mother talked about building bridges, others spoke about burning them."

Now he sounded bitter. His jaw was set and his face was flushed. For a moment no one spoke.

With an effort he calmed himself. "The best times we had were when your ma and I were alone. Just her and me. We lived undercover for one year, until your mother found out she was pregnant. That's when the fights began. Cat and dog we became. She wanted a father for you and could no longer accept our secrecy. She woke up one day and gave me the chop. Then she ran away – back to the farm. What's its name?"

"Milky Way."

"Ja, that's it," he nodded. "Melkweg. I followed your ma there. It was night when I arrived and the whole sky was filled with stars. I saw a light coming from one of the workers' rooms. I caught sight of the woman who lived there, explained who I was, and asked her to fetch Riana from the big house. That woman let me stay in her room."

"Lettie," Kim said. "That was Lettie who helped you." Kim bit her tongue and did not say what she was thinking – *She was banished from the farm for doing so.*

"Riana booked her ticket in less than a week," Hendrik said. He swallowed loudly and added. "Her mind was made up and off to Canada she went."

Kim did not know if she should be angry or sad. Instead, she kept her eyes fixed on the harbor. She traced with her eyes the route she imagined the tall ships took, coming around the Cape of Good Hope. Then she spoke.

"If you were in love why didn't you follow Riana to Canada? After all that had happened, why didn't you?"

Hendrik turned to her. "I was not as brave as your mother. What was Canada to me? Who was I to Canada? Nothing! I would stay and fight for South Africa to change! And when it did – when all those years of hard work and believing in victory paid off – I took my rightful place. How could I not take it?"

"Did you ever ask for a picture of me?" Kim asked.

"I wanted to contact you. So often I have lived this encounter in my mind and in my heart. But I couldn't risk that a newspaper might try to dig up the fact that I had a child – a white child – and was not the person I appeared to be." He forced himself to look at Kim. "I shouldn't have cared what people might think. But I did."

Kim continued to stare at the water. She wanted to find the exact place where the ultra marine blue ocean and the gray-green one, mixed one with the other. Kim had always believed that this bay was the precise spot where the two oceans met but recently Themba had told her that wasn't true. According to scientists, the meeting place – and the farthest tip of Africa – was farther to the east at Cape Agulhas. How many things in life are like this, thought Kim: you think it's one way, but it turns out to be a lie.

She turned back to Hendrik. *Am I still a secret?* Kim wanted to ask him. *Are you still afraid of what others will think of you? You and your white child?*

Hendrik read her expression. "I have told Ginger about you, and soon everyone will know," he said.

She focused again on the bay. Eventually she found what she was looking for. Beyond Robben Island was a long white line of breaker waves. Maybe the scientists were wrong and this was where the warm Indian waters collided with the cold Atlantic.

"Can we go down now?" she asked. "I've had enough."

"Of course," said Hendrik as he led them back to the cable station.

# TWENTY-ONE

# GOOD-BYES

"**Y**ou're disappointed in him, aren't you?" Themba said. He and Kim were kicking a soccer ball between them in the schoolyard as they waited, and he was slightly out of breath.

"What are you talking about?" Kim asked.

He frowned. "I'm talking about your father, your pa."

She booted the ball and he sprinted after it. For a few moments they passed it between them. Finally, Kim charged up to the goalpost and kicked the ball.

"He was okay," Kim said. "I told you. He's basically a nice guy. We just don't have an awful lot in common, that's all."

But it was hard to conceal her real feelings from Themba. He knew her too well.

"You think he should have dropped everything and followed your mom to Canada?" Themba asked.

She adjusted her sunglasses on her sweaty nose. "I don't know," she said.

"You think he should have given everything up to enter the white world of your mother?"

Kim jammed her heels into the hard earth and glared at him. The way he said *white world* reminded her of when Hendrik called her his *white child*.

"Sorry, hey," he said drawing close. "But you don't understand what it was like in those days. Young children fought with stones and bricks to defend what they believed to be theirs. Daily, people like my father were willing to die for liberation. This was Hendrik's country and he wanted to be here."

Kim did not respond. The sun, that had been partly hidden by the side of the school building, had shifted so that it drilled into the back of her head. She belted the ball back into the field. She was irritated. With the heat. With Themba. With Hendrik. With herself.

The week had gone fast since she and Hendrik had taken the cable car up Table Mountain. Afterwards she went home and collapsed on her bed. Riana had given Kim homeopathic tablets for upset stomach. But her stomach didn't hurt. Nothing hurt, really. She was entirely numb.

It was Lettie who unlocked the emotions that Kim needed to feel. She came in with sweetened tea and marmite smeared on large white crackers. She set the tray down and stood over the bunk bed to feel Kim's forehead.

For the first time, the full realization that they would be gone in less than a week, hit Kim. Tears burned the back of her throat. She wished Lettie and Themba could come back with them to Canada, but she knew her mother would never allow it.

"Will you soon visit Grandma Elsie and your sister at the farm?" Kim asked as she turned away. She didn't want Lettie to see how she chewed her lip to keep the tears in check.

"I am going to see them next weekend," Lettie responded.

It was hopeless. Kim could no longer hold on. She threw the covers back and pounded the mattress like a two year old. Then came a cry that began deep in her gut and vibrated through her body like a spasm. "Why don't you hate them?" she cried, tears streaming down her face. "All of them! My mom! Oupa! The policeman!"

Lettie laid a cold facecloth across Kim's forehead trying to calm her. "I have no heaviness toward your ma," she said. "She was brave, too. I lost my home at the farm, but I did gain a different life for my children. Toward your Oupa and that policeman, I am angry. But I try not to be bitter." She paused. "When you are bitter, you are lost." Kim had closed her eyes and let the facecloth cool her brow. Her heart stilled; her outburst had released something inside her.

Kim looked up and started. She remembered where she was. Themba was standing beside her with one foot on the soccer ball. The sun was very hot.

Themba took a brown paper bag from his rucksack and handed it to her. "Open this after I'm gone," he said. Then he packed the ball away.

"Where you going?" she asked.

Ignoring her question, Themba pointed across the street from the school and asked, "Is this them?"

Kim turned to look. The two figures were still a distance away, but Kim recognized Hendrik, tall and dignified in his trousers and light jacket. Beside him was a young girl with pigtails, in a cotton dress and long white kneesocks. They were waiting for the light to change.

"That's Hendrik and his daughter, Ginger."

Themba quickly flung his rucksack onto his back. "You need to see them alone."

"Stay!" she begged. "Don't you want to meet them?"

"No," Themba firmly shook his head. "This is between the three of you."

"Are you sure?" she pleaded.

"Yes. I'll call you later."

She wondered if she should hug Themba like her mother did with her journalist friends. Instead, she waited to see what he would do. He shook her hand folding the fingers one way and then the other – the African handshake. Then he hugged her – a quick one, but a hug, nevertheless.

"I got something for you too," Kim said as she pulled back. "It's from my mom and me."

Themba was still holding her hand. He gave her fingers a little squeeze. "Thank you," he said as he took the plastic bag.

"Don't open it now," Kim said.

But there was no danger of that. Themba had disappeared. He'd cut behind the street vendors and made his way toward home.

After a moment Hendrik and the young girl approached, but Kim couldn't help looking once more at the spot where Themba had disappeared.

"Kim, this is Ginger," said Hendrik.

"Hi," said Kim, finding her voice.

"Hey," said Ginger, in a pleasant voice, much like her father's. She was a slim girl with a big smile. "Is he your boyfriend?" she asked.

"Ginger," Hendrik warned. "Be polite."

"It's okay," Kim said with a laugh.

"Is he the friend who contacted me?" Hendrik asked.

Kim nodded. "He didn't want to impose on the time we have left."

They fell silent and started walking toward the Botanical Gardens. Trees formed an arch of green foliage over their heads as they walked down the lane. They could hear frogs croaking in the nearby ponds. In the middle of the gardens was an outdoor tearoom.

They selected a table on the edge of the terrace. Close by, noisy birds fluttered in cages. "When do you leave on the plane?" Ginger asked, after they had ordered their drinks.

It was so warm that Kim fanned herself with the menu. "Tomorrow night," she said.

"When will you come back?"

Kim thought about it for a second. "I don't know."

"Where's your ma?" Ginger asked.

Hendrik frowned at all the questions, but Kim answered patiently. "Working late, no doubt. She'll be here soon." She made herself look at the bird-cages behind her. She really wanted to stare at Ginger's skin and hair – compare them to her own – but she knew that would be rude. Themba's words: *The white world of your mom*, rang in her ears.

Hendrik poured out his tea. Beads of condensation formed on the side of Kim's Coke glass. "Ginger, Kim's mother has been covering the Truth and Reconciliation Commission. I told you about that."

Kim was relieved to have a topic to talk about. "This morning Mom sent off her final dispatch," she said. "*Whites Only signs are gone. Black and white children mix in schools. But the Pandora's Box, which was opened long ago, has put a spell on this country that will take generations to heal. This is Riana van der Merwe reporting from Cape Town, South Africa.*"

Hendrik laughed. "I can just hear her."

"What's a Pandora's Box?" Ginger asked.

"A girl called Pandora opened a box that she wasn't supposed to and all the troubles of the world flew out," Kim said.

"Your mother is right. There are many challenges ahead of this country," Hendrik said, stirring sugar into his tea.

"Why?" Kim asked picking up her Coke. "Why is it so hard for people to admit that they're wrong?"

Hendrik shrugged. "Ja. I suppose it's the hardest thing a person can do. To admit that everything upon which their life is built is false." For a second he didn't look at her. Then he added. "I was wrong, hey. I'm sorry. I shouldn't have let other people's definitions matter to me."

Kim looked into her father's eyes and saw a strange mix of warmth and regret. "Maybe one day I'll understand," she said.

The odd thing was, she *did* understand. Not everything, but more than she had before.

Riana rushed up to their table, flustered and on edge. As soon as she joined them Kim could see that. Hendrik was also tense, but, after Riana had ordered, he tried to get her to relax. "*Gee 'n bietjie vir my daai handjie,*" he said giving her hand a little squeeze.

"Ms van der Merwe, will you come back to South Africa soon?" Ginger asked politely.

"Well," Riana said with a tight smile, "I hope so." While they waited for the food to arrive, they spoke about the weather and how it had turned warm very quickly.

"We're not related," Ginger suddenly asked Riana, "are we?"

"No, but you and Kim are."

When the food arrived Hendrik joked about how, at this very restaurant, a gull had once made off with one of his fries. Riana laughed and Kim was relieved that she was beginning to respond to Hendrik's attempts to lighten things up.

At the end, Riana suggested paying for the meal. "*Nee*, man," Hendrik responded. "I'll pay." They made a joke of it. Riana holding the tab tightly between her fingers and Hendrik trying to grab it. Kim watched them as, giggling and whispering in Afrikaans, they both made their way to the cash register inside the tearoom.

After they were alone Ginger pointed to the gift Themba had given Kim. "What's in the parcel?" she asked.

"I don't know."

"Open it," said Ginger leaning closer to see.

Kim ripped off the paper. Themba's present was a clothbound notebook with a border of bright diagonal shapes. On the cover was the drawing of a turquoise guinea fowl with a polka dotted body and

a crimson headpiece. Under it, penned in a beautiful script, the word *Afrika*.

Ginger gasped in delight. "What's inside?" she
asked.

Kim twisted the clasp and opened the notebook. Themba had scribbled something on the
inside page. Ginger insisted on reading it out loud:
"One day I will visit your country, I promise. Thanks
for this friendship. Love, Themba."

Kim cradled the beautiful notebook in her
arms. She saw a pay phone on the corner of the
terrace and got to her feet.

"Ginger," she instructed. "Keep the gulls off my
fries."

Kim crossed to the phone and dialed. She
heard Themba's voice. Polite and surprised, he
shouted. "HELLO?"

"Themba, you nut, it's me. Does it work?"

"It's cool," Themba bellowed. "It's awesome, as
you would say. How did you talk your ma into
leaving it for me?"

"Stop shouting! I reminded her that a South
African cell phone won't work in Canada."

"It's perfect," he said in a normal voice. "I love
it."

"Thanks for the great notebook," Kim said,
through her blurred vision. She swallowed carefully
and added: "And thanks for finding Hendrik."

"Pleasure," Themba said. He cleared his throat.

"Something I didn't tell you," Kim said swallowing back the tears. "You were right. I was disappointed at first. But seeing him, talking to him, clears up so many questions I had about who I am."

"And the girl?" asked Themba.

Kim watched as Ginger skillfully diverted a seagull from picking up one of her fries. "She's fine. Very cute, actually." Kim's ear ached from holding the phone so tightly. "Will you really come and visit us in Canada?" she asked. "I know my mom could arrange it. You'll need a passport."

"I'll need a bearskin coat!" Themba said with a laugh.

Kim noticed Riana and Hendrik were still standing near the cash register talking together. Her mother had one hand on his forearm as if telling him something important.

"Will you call me before you leave tomorrow?" Themba asked.

"Yes," said Kim. "I won't say good-bye now." She felt a tear trickle down her cheek.

She hung up, rubbed the tear from her face, and crossed to where Ginger sat. "Thanks for watching my food," she said.

"My pleasure," said Ginger. The two girls finished off their fries in silence. *It isn't bad at all, having a half sister*, thought Kim.

Table Mountain was far above them. It was a pearly-gray color – very majestic in the summer light. She recalled the day she and Hendrik made the trip up to the top. She would remember this African mountain for as long as she lived.

Ginger pushed her plate away. "What are they doing?" Riana and her father were still near the cash register, but now they smiled and laughed together.

"She's pretty," said Ginger.

"He's handsome."

"He's married," added Ginger. "He's married to my mother."

"I figured that out," said Kim laughing, even though she hadn't thought about it.

Riana and Hendrik finally returned to the table. Riana was pale and her cheeks were streaked with tears. But she was smiling. "Took you long enough," Kim said.

"We thought you would never finish paying the bill," added Ginger.

Riana glanced across at Hendrik. She looked more relaxed than she had in months, maybe even years.

The girls rose to their feet and followed Riana and Hendrik out of the tearoom. Suddenly Ginger leaned closer to Kim as if telling her a secret. "Are you angry that I knew the truth about you before you knew the truth about me?" she asked. Her voice sounded grown up and formal, and Kim liked this about her.

"Knowing the truth matters," admitted Kim, as they walked into the heat of the garden. "But it's what we do with it that counts."

## ACKNOWLEDGMENTS

I am happy to have the opportunity to acknowledge the many people in South Africa who befriended me and introduced me to their beautiful and troubled country: Vida du Plessis, Marianne Thamm, Glynis Lopez, Edward Shalala, Synnove Skjelten, Wayne Morris, Christell Stander, Cassandra Parker, and Gill Conry-Taylor. I would especially like to thank Helena Scheffler, Anne Mayne, Freddie van Staden, Laurence Cramer, and Phillip Kakaza for their careful reading of the manuscript. Others graciously contributed feedback to the completion of this book: Claire Letemendia, Caro Soles, Florence Gibson, Constance Rennett, Marg Webb, Anne Perdue, Eva Tihanyi, Laurie Colbert, and Dominque Cardona. Heartfelt thanks to my editor, Kathryn Cole, my publisher, Kathy Lowinger, and my agent, Suzanne Brandreth. Most of all I would like to acknowledge Lynne Viola for love and support over the years and her expert editorial guidance in shaping this book.